Love
at
Eagle Station

The Inheritance Bay • Book Two

SUSAN WARNER

Love
at
Eagle Station

One

Layla Cartia was prone to making quick decisions and speaking her mind. Her brother assured her it would come to bite her on the rear one day, but after thirty-two years, she thought the probability of that happening was slim to none.

She needed to think and act quickly because she was a potter. Clay demanded action and a firm resolve. She had just finished a set of four bowls, and nothing gave her more satisfaction than looking at a finished piece of work. There was something to be said about making things with your hands. She was able to put a bit of herself into every piece she created. Layla liked to think that she imbued her clay works and pottery with a bit of herself.

Layla locked the front door of her shop, Clay Comforts. Her brother had been operating the front of the store most of the day, leaving her to take care of the bowls she had finally finished. Layla was a member of the Breeder Rescue Group. The little furball she took with her to the store was called Princess; the dog was a rescue

Yorkie. She had been raised in a puppy mill and had never been out of a cage. Now she was adjusting to walking and being able to just be a dog.

Layla was tired and would fall out on the couch she had put in the back of the store and go to sleep if her rescues weren't waiting for her at home. She knew her brother had put them in the guest bedroom, but they still needed some love, food, and hopefully, she would be able to get them to walk a little farther today. Some dogs raised in cages and puppy mills seldom got to walk outside of their cages, so getting a newly rescued dog to walk around could be a challenge. To help them, Layla always padded the surrounding area with padding and rugs so they could explore.

She couldn't wait until Princess was ready to see all of Inheritance Bay. The Bay itself was a source of peace and serenity for Layla. Her mother had arrived here with no past, and the town of Inheritance Bay had accepted her and her two children. Layla grew up a child of the Bay. She knew how to kayak on the bay, swim in the bay, frequent the picnic areas around the bay, and most of all, she knew how to take long naps on the grass under the evening stars. Layla loved the town that had accepted and raised her.

Things weren't going so well for the Bay area, though. Layla was an optimist, but she didn't turn a blind eye to her surroundings. Inheritance Bay barely got by on the tourist influx that happened only three months of the year. She did pretty well with her pottery abroad and in town, but the town needed more. Layla had heard that Marjorie had sent out some letters to ask people to come back to the Bay. Layla wasn't so sure how that was going to go, but she would be open-minded if it helped the town.

"Layla, you going home, child?" Mason Byers asked from across the street as he made his way down the block.

"Yes, I am, Mr. Byers. Make sure you take care of that limp," she replied. He smiled, waved her off, and moved on.

Layla smiled as she walked home. She was an integral part of the Bay. Everyone knew everyone here. They all accepted her, and most of the older people had helped raise her and her brother. Through good times and bad, the town stuck together to make it. Except maybe Conner Sanders. He had bought up land, but no one knew what he was going to do with it. His new fiancée, Riley, seemed like she was going to help him make some decisions, but Layla didn't like to get ahead of herself. She would wait and see how it all panned out.

"Have you decided to do your duty yet, girl?" a voice called out to her.

David Tasker—the only man who somehow thought she could single-handedly save Inheritance Bay. Layla closed her eyes and tried to think of something that would be calming. His house was on the way to hers, and she didn't know how he did it, but he always managed to be outside when she was going home.

"Mr. Tasker, funny that you should be out here this evening."

"I'm surprised you can see the problem and be unfazed. It must be a generational thing," he complained. Layla didn't want to give him the time of day, but she was raised with manners that overlooked the rudeness of elders. She couldn't remember a time when she had seen Mr. Tasker happy. When she had arrived with her mother at Inheritance Bay, Mr. Tasker's wife had already passed at a very young age, and Mr. Tasker was never the same.

His goal was to make Inheritance Bay the way it was when his wife was alive. Now, Mr. Tasker thought she was the way to make that happen.

"I hope you have a good day, Mr. Tasker," she said, making sure she was still moving as well as answering him.

"If you really meant it, you'd do what you should and bring your business to the Bay and let everyone know the famous potter lives here."

Layla didn't answer because she refused to have the same old argument with Mr. Tasker. It was true, she had found some level of success with her crafts, but she also valued her privacy. Her brother was just as well known for his skills as a potter, and he had tried to do the same thing. He was stalked until it caused an accident that left him with a limp and almost took his hands. When her brother had come out of the hospital, he made her promise never to put herself in that position.

Still, the accusation stung when she heard it from Mr. Tasker. She was caught between her promises to her brother and saving the place that had accepted her lone mother when it appeared she had nowhere else to go. The slam of Mr. Tasker's porch door with no spring gave her some relief that he had gone inside. While one pressure was gone, another resurfaced.

Another thing that weighed on her mind was the question of where her mother was from and why had she been alone with two children and finding her way here in Inheritance Bay?

Her thoughts were disturbed by the smell of steaks on the grill as she walked up to her house. Steaks? Layla looked and saw the beckoning plume of smoke rising from her next-door neighbor. When she opened the door to her home, she dropped her purse and went to check on her charges. She had three altogether. While the other two were asleep, Princess was standing, sniffing toward the screen door.

"You can smell it, too, huh?" Layla said. It smelled like a great skirt or T-bone steak, and from the smell of it, the person knew how to season it. She smelled the bold flavors of garlic, olive oil, and a little bit of chili powder. Sighing, she picked up a nearby basket and then picked up Princess and put her in it. Layla knew everyone, and she knew that whoever was next door was a visitor to the area.

"Let me see if I have a Welcome to Inheritance Bay cup, and if so, we can get the introductions out of the way. Our neighborly duty will be done, and it will be a bit of air for you tonight. The walker texted her daily report, you didn't feel like walking like the other dogs and had to be carried today but don't worry, I'm sure tomorrow you'll be more open to the experience," she said to Princess.

Layla walked out of the front of her home to see a shiny sports car in the driveway next door. She shook her head and smiled to herself. *It looks like someone hasn't heard about seawater and fancy cars*, she thought.

So, whoever was next door was more than likely a snowbird. Snowbirds were city folk who came to get away and then went home. Layla remembered the council saying they would open up some houses for rental to raise cash, but she hadn't realized it was the house next to hers. Layla shrugged. She guessed it made sense, though, as she lived in a cul-du-sac conveniently located in the midst of town.

She had her mug in one hand and Princess in a basket in the other. She was sure she was the epitome of small-town charm, knocking on the door. After she knocked, her cell phone rang. Unable to answer it, she let it go to voicemail, but then it buzzed. So, she looked on her smartwatch to see the text *DO NOT GREET THE NEIGHBOR!* from her brother.

Just as she was about to turn away, the door opened.

"Really, I'm not here two hours, and I'm getting crank doorbell rings."

The man sounded annoyed, and Layla was insulted that he thought that was what was going on. She wouldn't go into his house, but she wasn't going to run, either.

"It's not a doorbell crank. I decided to be neighborly," Layla replied. The man was about six foot one with curly black hair and a well-shaped beard that seemed so in style these days. With blue eyes, a square jaw, and what looked like a dimple in his chin, he could have been gorgeous if not for that attitude.

"Neighborly? You mean nosy," he said gruffly.

"Nosy! Wow, I should have listened to my instincts and went back home."

"Aw, come on. I know how these small towns work. When I came over that bridge into town, all the elderly women had their dentures clacking about who I was and what I'm doing here."

"You are so full of yourself. I, for one, don't know who you are or why you're here, and I don't care. Also, for your information, the elderly women are not gossips; they are some of the nicest women you could know. Although, you might push even them to not be as charitable as they usually are."

"So, you're saying no one told you about me?" he said with a smirk, and his arms covered his well-made chest if the shape of his shirt could be trusted.

"I—" Layla stopped the denial that was coming to her lips. Then she saw him smile triumphantly, and the dimple on his cheek that was only a hint deepened true.

"I knew it. They sent you!"

"Stop, they didn't send me. They told me too late not to talk to you, and I have to say if you are this prickly with everyone, I can understand."

"You mean, you don't know who I am?"

Layla rolled her eyes and then remembered she had the cup. "Listen, I don't care. Here, take the cup. Welcome to Inheritance Bay, and may your stay be short!" she said as she pushed the cup into his hand and turned with Princess in her basket. Princess, of course, was trying to look at the man. There was no accounting for Princess's taste.

"Hey, my name is Nolan Taggert and—"

"Really, Mr. Taggert, that's nice that you can say your name, but I don't need it. You can have a nice life and vacation. We don't need to speak. We don't need to say hello. We don't need to interact at all because—"

"Would you please let me finish my sentence!"

Layla turned and found Mr. Taggert right behind her on her driveway on the way to her house. "Well, I can't

11

see how the sentence would matter either way, but—"

"I'm Nolan Taggert, and I work for Conner Sanders, the Wealth Builders owner and owner of one-third of this town. I've come to see if it's worth saving or not. Do I have your attention now?"

Layla turned to look at a smug Nolan Taggert standing in her driveway, and the only thing she could think was that her brother was right about her quick attitude and quick mouth. Nolan Taggert was the man who had come to deliver the bite.

Two

"Well, you have my attention; the question is, are you going to say anything worthwhile, or are you just good at one-liners? Of course, there is nothing wrong with one-liners, but a man should know his limits," she said.

"I didn't catch your name," Nolan said.

"I didn't give it," Layla replied. She felt her watch vibrate, and she could see it was her brother. She clicked on the return message *I'm busy*. She turned back to the problem at hand. "So, are you going to explain how you would single-handedly save the town of Inheritance Bay from whatever perceived threat you think is out there?"

She knew who Wealth Builders were, which was the only reason she even gave him the time of day. He was not the vision she would have come up with as a knight in shining armor. However, Layla was a big proponent of not judging a book by its cover.

"Your name?" he persisted.

"Layla Cartia, resident artist, and a Bay resident. Now

that we have the pleasantries done, can you answer the question?"

"Hello, Ms. Cartia—"

"Layla."

"Excuse me, I—"

"Only my mother was called Ms. Cartia. Everyone in town calls me Layla. It's the name on my art, and it's what I go by. You can call me Layla."

"Well, Layla, thank you for the welcome."

Oh, she wanted to rip the smile off of his face. It made it worse that the man was twice as attractive with a smile on his face than he was with the grimace from a moment before. When he smiled, his whole body relaxed. Where before he seemed like he would explode any minute, he now looked like he could invite a person out to dinner. His smile reached his eyes, where she saw the familiar crow's feet. Laughter was no stranger to his face if the laugh lines were to be used as a gauge.

"So, are you going to tell me how you intend to do this miracle and single-handedly save the town?"

"Not today, no. I have to meet with the mayor in the morning. After that, I'll know what I want to say to everyone."

Layla smiled and nodded her head. "You know what? I don't think you have any idea what it would take to save the town or how much damage your employer has done here," Layla fired back.

"My employer, Conner? You've got it all wrong, you see—"

"All wrong? No, Mr. Taggert, you've never had it right. This town has been in duress for years, barely holding on to its charm. The people are hardworking and caring. Then one day, a big corporation like yours comes in and buys up buildings and land that we were going to try to renovate to bring in income and, in a moment, months of planning was gone and with it our hopes. So, to hear that your company sent a henchman to see what can be done, I'm just not as impressed as you may think I should be."

"Why put the buildings on the market? It's not Conner's fault the town is in this situation. You see, if they had—"

Layla held up her hand to stop him from talking and then waved goodbye to Nolan.

"Well, I'd like to stay here and hear you justify your boss's behavior, but I have things to do," she said as she carried Princess back to the house.

"You know you can come over any time. For you, I'd take time out of my schedule, Layla Cartia."

Layla turned and looked at him. "I would love to say it was a pleasure, but it was anything but."

"You wound me, Layla."

"Get thicker armor. Good day, Nolan Taggert, and by the way, welcome to Inheritance Bay."

Nolan went back into his home. She was right; he was surly. The door had closed, but he was ever prepared. He had a spare key under the welcome mat. He took his first gift from the area and went to sit in his backyard. He

15

didn't really do backyards. Backyards were for families, and he was a condominium kind of man. However, the opportunity to make a steak made him overlook those inhibitions. He took the mug and placed it on the side table next to the lounge chair he was sitting in.

This was the place that most people aspired to visit and wished they could stay. A small community where everyone knew everyone. The sky seemed as though it stayed endlessly clear. The town's sounds had a rhythm of their own and coincided with the rising and the setting of the sun. The house he was staying in was inland, but it was one of the taller homes in the area. While most houses just had two stories, this rental had an extra floor put on it so that he could rent the attic out if he owned it. The attic apartment had a veranda, and according to the realtor, had been owned by the wife of a smuggler. He built the veranda so she could see the bay to know when he returned. Later a bunch of eagle conservationists, having heard the story came to the house and called it Eagle station.

Small towns had stories to up the value of their houses and disguise the lack of privacy. Although, he had to admit that he had been on that veranda and had seen Inheritance Bay during sunrise. An eagle had flown by to pluck its dinner from the bay. It was humbling and made him realize how unique the location could be. He was surprised he could see any town with that type of open-mindedness.

Nolan's experience with small towns was nowhere near as idyllic. He normally saw them for what they were, shells to hold a group of people who would decide who fit and who didn't. They didn't usually like strangers, and the rumor mill could be a vicious place if you managed to upset the wrong people.

He closed his eyes, laid his head back, and wondered why he had even bothered to come to the town. He could have looked at all of the data from his office and come to the same conclusions. Why had Conner wanted him to physically come here? To be fair, Nolan had to acknowledge he could have said no. He knew he was a lot of things, but being objective wasn't one of them when it came to small towns.

All of those truths, yet here he was, sitting in the backyard on a nice evening with a handmade mug beside him. He smiled. Yes, the mug that had come from the clear-spoken neighbor who seemed very transparent in her dislike of him. Nolan was used to people hiding the fact.

Hiding. That wasn't something Nolan did or appreciated in others. Maybe he needed to stop hiding from his thoughts on small towns. Perhaps this was a chance for him to see if he could be objective and keep his personal feelings out of the matter. Obviously, Conner thought so.

"Go to Inheritance Bay. It has a way of growing on you," Conner had said.

"Gangrene, leeches, and tumors do, as well, but no one tells you to encourage those," Nolan had replied.

Conner had thought he was joking, but he wasn't. Ever since Conner fell in love, he had an idealistic vision that all things could be fixed. Nolan was waiting for the love glow to dissipate before suggesting that something associated with Riley or her dog might not be perfect, especially the town she called home.

Nolan didn't hate Inheritance Bay. He didn't know Inheritance Bay. At first glance, it looked like a postcard, but it brought up such memories in him of his hometown—or the place he would have called his hometown if his mother hadn't needed to give him up for adoption to stay in it.

To add insult to injury, when Nolan looked as though he was going to try to wiggle out of the duty, Conner said that going to Inheritance Bay could be like a vacation for him. At the thought of vacation, his hand tightened on the mug. He took a look at it and could tell it was sturdy and well-made.

Even though his neighbor didn't know him, he knew who she was as soon as she said her name. Nolan had researched the whole town and knew that the potters lived there. He didn't understand why they didn't advertise the fact, but he knew who she was.

He had already met with the mayor of the town. Nolan had to say he wasn't impressed. The man was an elderly gentleman, but he seemed ready to say anything to get him to believe that the town was a good investment. Nolan didn't think Layla would do that.

Just thinking about her brown curly hair next to those high cheekbones and smooth skin made him lose his focus. When she spoke, color came rising into her face making her look like a goddess on fire. He wondered if it was just because she was angry, or did she get that way about everything she was passionate about?

Layla was a woman who stood her ground against greater odds. He didn't mind that. In fact, right now, it was refreshing. Honesty was hard to come by. He shouldn't be shocked by her reaction. What had he expected when he told her he was here to save the town?

It didn't matter. The reason he was here wasn't going to change. He had a job to do, and he was going to do it to the best of his ability despite an enticing neighbor with a bold personality.

Three

Layla woke from a long night of weird dreams involving a pushy neighbor who walked around with no shoes outside of his house. When she woke, her brother, Ryan, was at the door to pick up her other two charges. After retelling her experience with Nolan, her brother shrugged and warned her she should pick up her phone more often and stay away from tall, dark, and combative men. When Ryan reached for Princess, she growled, and Layla's brawny brother said Yorkie bites hurt the worst. That was the end of that conversation and the exodus of Ryan and her two charges.

After settling Princess down, Layla needed to destress. She decided to take a walk and left out the back of her house. It had nothing to do with the sports car in front of her neighbor's house. She just needed to have some alone time.

She walked until she was on the beach, which was about a twenty-minute walk from her house. She went down the pathway and then took off her shoes as her feet sunk into the warm sand. The water lapped up on the beach bringing with it kelp and tiny sea creatures. As the tide went out, it took with it some of the creatures that had hitched a ride and others that had waited for a wave to take them out.

There were a couple of other people walking along the beach. They just gave each other a nod, neither party wanting to disturb their morning communion. A couple of seagulls flew above, looking for leftovers that had undoubtedly been left by last night's partying high schoolers.

Everywhere she looked, she saw a good, clean life where someone would be grateful to have grown up and to live there still today. Things hadn't been smooth when she and Ryan had arrived, but things could have been worse. She and her family could have found a town that ran her mother out instead of welcoming her into their lives.

Inheritance Bay had accepted Layla's mother and seen a woman who was trying to do the best she could do by herself. She had no other family, and she wouldn't talk about where she had come from.

The town as a whole had been put in a position that was hard at best. Her mother had no ID but insisted she wasn't illegal. They had taken her at her word and given her a job and housed her children. Layla and Ryan had United States birth certificates and social security numbers, so getting them in schools and care with the doctors was no issue, but that wasn't the case for Layla's mother. She would pay for all of her care in cash, and she asked everyone in the Bay to respect that. It took a special kind of town to do that, and they had.

Layla could feel the heat of the morning sun on her face drying the tears of gratefulness that had fallen unbidden. She took a deep breath and headed back to the house. She glared at the house next door to her. Who would be so narrow-minded as to paint all small towns the same way? Oh, that would be Nolan Taggert, the town saver. She didn't know what his deal was with small towns, but it wasn't going to go well for the Bay if he had the final word.

As she continued to her house, she debated if she should go through the front or the back. She decided to return the way she had left. It was just less hassle, was all. In no way was she trying to avoid the town saver. She was about to her backyard gate when she stopped with her hand on the gate lock. The house next door never had dogs, so the fence was low, and the slats were spread apart, just enough to see her neighbor coming into his backyard.

His hair was slicked back and wet. Tiny droplets of water falling to his shoulders. He had on a stained, torn tee-shirt that played peek-a-boo with muscles beneath. The shirt said he was working, and his jeans hung low on his hips with a belt buckle that was turned to the right side of his hips.

He had a wrench in one hand and her cup in the other. He placed the wrench down and then rubbed the back of his neck. Then he brought her mug to his lips and drank long and deep. Whatever was in the cup clearly wasn't hot, as he swallowed it down, making his Adam's apple move with each gulp. Then he closed his eyes, put the mug down, and reached up as if he would somehow hug the sun. Layla thought, looking at those arms, he might be able to entice the sun to lean a little closer to him.

The fall of the latch broke the spell and had her shaking her head over her episode. She didn't even know what to call it. When she looked up, there he was, peering back at her as if he, too, were taking his fill. She had never felt so conscious of shorts and a tank top. She was glad she had the wrap on, but it did nothing to make her feel more covered. Determined not to be the one to make the moment any more awkward than what it already was, she nodded and then went into her yard, grateful for the tall walls.

When she opened her glass door and walked in, Princess lifted her head, stretched her body in a full extension, and then went to the glass door.

"You're too late, sister. I'm sure he's gone inside by now. The show is over."

Princess gave her another look, and when it was clear Layla was not going to open the door, she went back to her bed and curled up.

"I'm getting changed, and then we are off to the store, lady. You need some socialization with good people, and you'll find nothing but that in the Bay," Layla said.

About an hour later, Princess was in her tote bag, with her pillow, leash, and collar, and they were on their way to Layla's first stop of the day, the Lighthouse Diner. This was where Layla got her first coffee and bagel, as well as the place her mother used to work before she died.

The town of Inheritance Bay could be summed up in downtown. It was five parallel blocks that showed all the Bay had to offer and on the third block on the right side was the diner. It had a steeple on the top of it that was rivaled only by the steeple atop her neighbor's house. Layla shook her head to move the images of Nolan Taggert from her brain. She had to admit he could wake a woman up like no cup of coffee could, and to think, he did it looking like a grease monkey. Layla guessed he did more than just drive that pretty ride in the front.

She was in front of the Lighthouse Diner, and she looked up to see the faux lighthouse on the face of it. She turned to find the nearest light pole and then took out Princess and her pillow. She put the pillow down with Princess atop it. She tied the leash loosely to the pole and connected it to Princess's leash. Princess looked at her as if she couldn't believe she was being left and then laid her head down.

"Sorry gal, no pets in the diner, but I'll bring a tasty, healthy scrap for you," Layla said.

When she walked into the lighthouse, it was like walking into her second home. In a moment, she was once again that nine-year-old girl who was welcomed by all. The booths were red vinyl with the same mini jukeboxes in each booth that ran on quarters, and the floors were black and white alternating boxes. The Lighthouse was a staple. The morning crowd was in, and the smell of pancakes, oatmeal, and the hand presser's whirring making fresh orange juice, was in high gear.

Several people nodded or waved at her. It was the perfect way to start a day. The lighthouse not only served all meals, but it was also the equivalent of the Inheritance Bay social center. If there was any news to be discussed, someone would be talking about it in the Lighthouse.

"So lookee here, Red came to get some food before she goes into the hole."

"Good Morning, Edgar." Layla made the time to speak to Edgar Harrington. He was the spirit of Inheritance Bay. Edgar was a widow and had been here for as long as she could remember. When she was younger, he would always catch her and nicknamed her red-handed or Red for short. Her mother spoke kindly of him, and more than once, he had picked up Ryan and herself from school to bring them to her mother here. He never had anything but kind words to say, but sometimes he would stare a little long into the distance. He was a man who had lost, but still, he had a smile for everyone.

"I'm thinking of starting a new series, and you are going to be my inspiration. I'm thinking to call it, Contentment."

"Girl, find a real subject. If you base it on me, you might get three pieces: me awake, me asleep, and me eating."

Next to him was his barstool buddy, Allen Patters, and he always had something to say.

"Red, I think I saw you taking a walk this morning, without your charges. Was that you?"

Allen had been the editor of the local paper when she was a teen. As the internet progressed, his paper was bought out and made digital. Since then, he did the same job he did before, gathering all the town info. The only difference was if you wanted the latest edition, you had to come to the Lighthouse to get it.

"It was me, Allen. You just want me to take Princess and the rest of them with me, so I have to go slow enough for you to send your hound out to play. I'm on to your tricks about not wanting to get the dog walker to take them to the park if they can play with my charges for free," she joked with him. Edgar laughed and nudged Allen.

"Oh, she done caught you there, Allen. Caught you well and good."

Layla laughed and looked at her watch. There wasn't any actual crime in the Bay, but she didn't want to leave Princess for too long.

She made it to an empty spot at the bar, and coffee in a ready-to-go cup appeared. Blake Severs pushed the cup closer to Layla. She had been here since her mother had come. She remembered Blake and her mom talking like school children. At first, the Bay residents were a bit distant but accepting of her mother, but their decision to embrace her mother was mainly due to Blake. She saw something in her mom that made them thick as thieves.

"So, have you heard the news?" Blake asked as she placed her hand around the coffee cup, effectively holding it hostage until she answered.

"I haven't heard, but I think I'm about to."

"The word is that the mayor was in talks with some guy from Wealth Builders. You'd think Conner Sanders would talk to the mayor himself, but no, he sent a lackey. The mayor said the lackey is renting the house next door to yours."

That was when it happened. The whole diner went silent. Layla hadn't witnessed this event since someone said Lucy Bindel had run off in the middle of the night, leaving her parents a note that said she was going to find herself.

"Has that lackey made any passes at you, Red? You know I'm not as young as I was, but I still got some fight in me. He won't be taking advantage of one of our own," Allen said as he stood up and placed his frail arm around Layla's shoulders. Allen said that big corporations always sent their lackeys just like they did when they bought his paper. "I don't even know why he bothered to rent anything in this town. How long does it take to say no?" Allen grumbled.

"We'll all just have to wait and see what actually happens. Sometimes it's not up to us but to whatever fate delivers," Edgar said with a soft smile as he looked at Layla.

"Yes, it's true, he is next door to me, but that is about all I can tell you. We met yesterday as I was coming back. I've seen him in his backyard dirty from working on his car, but that is about it. Maybe he likes driving to places instead of flying, so he rented. Look, I don't know."

"You say he was dirty from working on his car?" Edgar asked. At that moment, she saw the awareness in his eyes and a measuring that was going on that she had no idea about.

"Yes, it's some sort of sports car. It was black and low to the ground. The inside looked like tan leather."

"Oh, leather interior, and he was dirty, but she didn't see no dirt in the car, did you Red?" Allen asked.

Layla shook her head negatively.

"That takes some skill and care to keep that kind of leather clean," Edgar agreed.

"What exactly does a man's car have to do with anything?" Blake asked. "We don't want to know how

27

he's going to transport himself around town. We want to know what he is going to do or not do for the town."

"I'm not sure he can do anything," Layla said. "Before we all start jumping ship or saying he's our great hope, we need to find out how his meeting goes with the mayor," she said.

"Well then, let me not keep everyone in suspense."

Four

Layla closed her eyes and let out a deep breath. When she looked at the door, it was exactly who she hoped it wasn't, and to add insult to injury, he had Princess in his arms. Until that moment, Layla never realized how attractive a well-muscled man in a dress shirt and black pants could look with a small dog in his arms. It was such a dichotomy of looks that it made you look twice as if any woman needed another reason to take another look at Nolan Taggert.

There was an air of expectation in the diner that could be set off by any little thing. It was the first time that she had been in the town and seen people's attitude be anything less than friendly.

"It seems like I have the answers that everyone is waiting for. Is anyone bold enough to ask me?"

Layla looked at him and shook her head. Was he trying to start a riot? She walked away from the bar and went to stand in front of him.

"Can you at least try to behave now?" she murmured.

Then she stood up straighter and turned to face the diner. "Everyone, this is Nolan Taggert, and he's here with Wealth Builders to evaluate Inheritance Bay."

Edgar turned from Nolan and went back to his coffee, murmuring all the way.

"He's here to evaluate, my foot," he pondered just loud enough for Nolan to hear him, so Layla thought. She was proud of the older man having enough gumption to say something. It was odd, as a town, they all stuck together, but now she could see that they fell apart when they weren't reminded about a common cause.

Allen patted his friend on the back and then turned to Nolan.

"You've got yourself a car up at the Eagle's place, is that right?" Allen asked.

"I do. A Dodge Viper GTS. She gets me places."

"You bought it, or you fixed it?" Edgar asked.

"I did the cosmetic work, but she deserved nothing but the best to work on her engine, so I found the most qualified men. I was hoping to take a spin today after I spoke to your mayor."

"There's a strip of road at the end of town for cars like yours. It's got enough space for a machine that needs to let loose. Ask Layla; she knows."

"Thanks for the heads up. I had some business anyway, and this will work out simply fine."

Layla listened and couldn't believe what was happening. She wanted to grab Princess from Nolan and then walk out the front door and walk back in the Lighthouse. A few moments ago, they were all suspecting him of who knew what kinds of crime, and now they were offering her as a personal chaperone to see the sights.

Certainly, she wasn't the only one who didn't see past his chameleon-like nature?

"I came in here for a couple of things, and it turned out the mayor was right. He told me that most of the things and the people that I would be looking for would be here in the diner this time of day."

Edgar laughed. "Well, he got that right at least."

Blake came around the counter and nodded him toward a booth.

"You can take the one in the back, and Layla will put the baby in her bag. I don't know why she leaves her out there. Every one of us was a farmer or has dogs that are closer than our family."

Layla looked at Blake and, for once, couldn't believe her traitorous behavior. Didn't they remember who this man was? He was the one who had come to take away their treasured way of life. As he handed her Princess, Layla had to bite her tongue. Then she looked up into Nolan's face and smiled courteously.

"I'll take Princess and sit with you for a moment, but I don't want to take advantage of Blake's hospitality."

When he handed Princess over, she tried not to be offended by the Yorkie's forlorn look when she was given to Layla. It amazed her a man of his size would be so gentle with Princess. What was even more telling was the fact that Princess didn't mind being held by Nolan. Layla believed that animals, and dogs, in particular, were good judges of character.

Nolan Taggert as a whole package was distressing. He worked for Conner Sanders, and they both worked in finance. They should have looked like roly-poly accountants. In her head, they should have favored Mr. Potato's head in shape.

Then she remembered him this morning and the way he looked in his backyard. That was not the look of a man shaped like a potato or a bowling pin. It looked like a man who knew what he wanted, how to get it, and wasn't afraid to put in the work for it. Then he turned toward her, closed his eyes, and smiled.

"So, this morning were you going out or coming in?" he asked.

Layla hoped the morning sun and wind had done their part and given her a glow so that her embarrassment didn't show on her face. He would bring it up, no gentleman would bring it up, but that just told her all she needed to know.

"I was coming back. I try to get my me time in early because my day is usually hectic and unpredictable."

One side of his mouth ticked up. It didn't get to a full smile, but she could see the smirk on his face.

"My days are like that, too, so I like to do things that center me in the morning. You see, we have some things in common after all."

Layla plastered a smile on her face as she stroked the top of Princess's head in the bag.

"I think there is a distinctive difference. I wake to see my neighbors and get them on their way. You, on the other hand, make people run into their houses and hide." Layla wasn't going to drink the Nolan Taggert Kool-Aid. "Look, thank you for bringing in Princess, but I'm not comfortable with her being in the diner. Tourists come, and some are very finicky. You said you were here to take care of business, so I'll leave you to it."

"You are part of my business, Layla."

"What are you talking about?" Layla asked in a low huff.

"I need to tell you what I talked about with the mayor and how I plan to save your town."

"First of all, I've heard nothing that even suggests you want to save the town, much less how."

Nolan sat back in the booth. "So are you suggesting I'm not a man of my word, Layla? Be careful. I've actively hunted men who have accused me of similar things with no proof."

She sat back, Princess's head in front of her chest. "I'm sorry for voicing my concerns, but I like to make sure all parties know where we all stand. So, what do you want with me? I still have to earn a living, you know."

Nolan let out a big breath. "Well, the truth of it is, I'm good friends with Conner. Now that he's with Riley, he's become biased to this area, so he asked me to come and take a look and then evaluate if it's worth spending money on."

Layla got ready to give him a swift retort when she took a breath and tried to find her center as she stroked the top of Princess's head.

"Okay, spill it. What is it that you are doing because Conner can't? Just cut to the chase, so I can get to work."

She watched Nolan look around the diner and then at her. "I might be able to give an analysis of the town and see what its money-making potential is as a tourist spot."

Layla heard the hope in his words for her town. "You might?"

Nolan tapped the table. "Listen, Layla, I'm talking about giving the town a second chance, but I don't want the town to think it's a given thing. I need to evaluate them honestly first before I make that decision. So far, you are the most honest person in town, so I've decided that some time with you might give a good view of the town."

She waited for the other shoe to drop. "Okay, let's say I agree. What does your say-so mean for the town?"

"It means a redo, a start over. You could make Inheritance Bay into a tourist site, so the town would have a second chance," he said.

"A second chance for what? I'm not helping you turn the Bay into one of those places that sell their peace of mind for a dollar."

"Nothing so extreme. It would be a combination of two things. We, Wealth Builders, would help you with attracting tourists. We are looking to open a call center here, and I need to see what those potential employees would be walking into. Riley was determined that the town get an opportunity to fight for itself."

Layla nodded and once again thanked the fact that opposites attracted, and Conner was getting married to a sweet woman, Riley, who was his total opposite.

"It all sounds good, like you may have a plan. What do you need from me? Didn't you just meet with the mayor? He must have been thrilled, and he'll show you around."

"He was, and the way he described things, I would have told him no within fifteen minutes, if that long."

"You are being dramatic," she hissed. "The tone is all

the same, and you probably make him nervous. He's an older man."

"Well, I can't trust the voice of a person who is changing what the town is about in an attempt to say the town is about whatever I say," he replied.

Layla inwardly winced. She knew exactly what Nolan was talking about. It was actually one of the things people joked about. If the mayor had one feel about an issue, but you made it seem like that wasn't something you agreed with, he would soon change his mind. Layla supposed if you weren't exposed to it every day, it could seem sweet, but having to deal with it every day, she could see how it could be wearing, and it would aggravate Nolan.

"Okay, I hear you, but again, I'm having a hard time understanding what any of this has to do with me? You met with the mayor, and I'm sure he had a lot to say, and you told him what you are saying to me, and then the two of you made a plan."

Layla let her words sink in, and as Nolan listened, she watched him relax.

"Stop it already. What do you need to tell me?" she hissed.

He leaned forward and gave her a large smile.

"I told the mayor I wanted an honest person, and he elected you to be my town guide."

She didn't even have a response to his words. Could it be that the mayor had really sold her out like that? Layla had a sneaky suspicion as she watched the smile grow on Nolan's face that he was telling the truth.

"Why would you even agree to such a thing?" she asked Nolan.

"In the grand scheme of things, I happen to agree with him. From the first day that I arrived in this town, everyone has gone out of their way to be nice to me or to be nosy. You, Layla, are the only one who has been your true self."

"So, I get to be me, and you get to judge the whole town based on my personality?"

Nolan sat back in the booth and nodded his head.

"Well, that seems like a whole lot of pressure to put on one person."

"Inheritance Bay is like every other small town I have ever seen, Layla. It looks pretty on a postcard. It's got its characters and central meeting ground. If that was all it took for Wealth Builders to put up a center, I could have found a smaller town anywhere. My job is to make sure that if we put a center here, it is going to be an enriching experience for our employees. I think the only way that I can really find that out is to find out why someone who could live anywhere—because I know your artwork does well—chooses to stay here."

Layla wanted to argue with him and say that the reason she stayed had more to do with her mother than anything else. However, she could see by the way he was looking so self-satisfied that if he believed this was why she stayed, it would give him a good basis for the rest of the town.

"And what happens if I choose not to be your guide?" Layla asked.

"Then I'll pack up my bags, throw everything into the back of my car, and go back home. I'll let Connor know that this is not a viable site."

"I really think this is a little extreme. I mean, you should just go ahead and do the right thing because Connor lives here."

"You wouldn't be the first one to say that. But I try to make sure that when I make decisions about money, it has nothing to do with my feelings."

"I can't just drop everything and show you around today, so we're going to have to pick up after I get things settled, ok?"

"Of course, I'm here at your convenience."

"My convenience? If it were really that, you would be jumping off a bridge somewhere."

Nolan chuckled. "You're not the first person to have that sentiment, and you probably won't be the last. I look forward to seeing Inheritance Bay. Oh, and by the way, I do have a condition, Layla."

"Wow, first you make demands, railroad me into helping you, and now you've got conditions. Ok, what else?"

"What you are doing for the town by showing me about, no one but us can know what your end goal is or why I'm here. If anyone asks, you just need to say you're showing a friend of Connor's around."

"Are you serious?"

"Very much so. If everybody knows why I'm here, they'll change the way that they are by trying to make themselves into something that they're really not."

"Well, I think you should have thought about this a little bit better before you went to talk to the mayor. The rumor is that man talks in his sleep."

"I don't think I need to worry about the mayor. Wealth Builders made a sizeable contribution to the city."

"Already with throwing the money around," Layla sighed.

"Don't worry, Layla, this will be over before you know it," Nolan said.

Layla didn't even bother trying to be polite and say goodbye. She was sure that all of the eyes were on her as she walked out of the diner. What would she possibly tell them? *I just made a deal with the devil, and I can't tell you what it is*? No, Layla didn't have any idea what she was going to do, but she was going to think of something. She was going to save the town that had saved her and her brother and make Nolan Taggert fall in love with Inheritance Bay.

Five

Nolan was sure from the firm way Layla walked out of the diner that this was going to be an enjoyable encounter. He wasn't sure that anyone could say or do anything that would make him think that one town would be any better than the other, but he had told Connor he'd come and give it a go.

Layla was a formidable woman that intrigued him. Under different circumstances, Nolan could see that he and Layla might have had a different kind of relationship. He knew that she was personally invested in this town. However, what Layla didn't know was that Nolan always made decisions based on the numbers. Nolan had already looked at Inheritance Bay's numbers, and they didn't add up the way he needed them to in order for him to move a center here.

Pointing out that the town was just like so many other towns was just to make sure they were on the same playing field. The part that Nolan had not told her was that this town brought back memories. It brought back memories of a little boy who wasn't accepted and was sent away because of the prejudices of a small town.

Not even the night song of the cricket could take away the sting of rejection from his past. Lying in bed at night, the numbers regarding Inheritance Bay making a good investment wasn't what went through his head. It was whether or not the people were the same kind of people who would reject a little boy.

"Is Layla coming back?" The waitress asked as she refilled his coffee. He could tell that she really wanted to know so much more. Her eyes furtively glanced along the table, looking for any clues about what he was doing or what he had been talking about. This was the behavior he was used to in small towns. Nolan angled his head so he could read her name tag.

"Hello Kim, thank you so much for asking. But I will be finishing up my breakfast alone."

She gave him a quick nod and then moved on as if exasperated by her forwarded effort. He knew they were all aware that he was here to make some kind of judgment. It made it extremely hard to evaluate a town that was always on guard. Reading high tensions in a town was pretty easy. As soon as they stopped being nice and polite and offering suggestions, you knew you were on the wrong side of the town. No matter how nice Kim might be, she had totally forgotten to take his order or offer him the specials for the morning. At this point, Nolan thought he better be happy that he had gotten coffee while Layla was here.

Nolan looked into his coffee cup and wondered what he was doing here. He had walked into a lion's den of his past blindly. He was going to pay for his coffee and then leave. There was no sense in making this more of a painful encounter for Kim than it needed to be. He picked up his spoon and stirred his coffee one more time, looking for something or some kind of answer to his past and maybe his future, too.

His thoughts were interrupted by a familiar voice.

"The way you're looking into that coffee, it seems like there's gold. If you find some, don't forget to share with your old man."

Nolan looked up, but he knew who it was even before he saw the man's face. It was the voice that had raised him and taught him all he knew about being a man—his foster father, Colin Dent.

Colin Dent was a man among men. He was the one who took him in and raised him by himself. He had black hair with strands of gray weaving through the sides. Nolan remembered the first day he met Colin. At first, he had gone to him as a foster child. When Nolan arrived, he was sure that he had just been adopted because he had a strong back, and Colin needed help on his farm. It was only as the years went on that Nolan would discover that Colin didn't need any help whatsoever. This single man had taken him and raised him to be the man he was today. It was true, he used to receive a monthly check for him as a foster child, but it in no way covered everything that Colin had done for him.

Colin had sent him to a private school. Colin had given him a tutor when it seemed as though he had trouble with his subjects. And when Nolan had turned eighteen, Colin thought every man should see the world, and he sent him on a two-week trip to go see the continents at a glance.

More importantly, he was the one who had encouraged Nolan to find his mother. The relationship between the two of them had never been very strong. Ellen Anders, his mother, was a complicated woman. These days she went by her maiden name, Ellen Taggert. She could make you believe she was the happiest person on the planet. She could hide what she was really feeling in order to fit into a town that she never wanted to leave. But those were memories that Nolan didn't want to look at.

Nolan stood up and pulled Colin into a bear hug. "What are you doing here?"

"So much for asking me how my trip was or where I'm staying. Kids always start out with, why are you here? It's why we all think that kids are always in trouble."

What could Nolan say? Here he was sitting in the middle of a small town trying to decide the fate of so many when he had so much personal baggage.

"I'm so sorry, take a seat, take a seat. Let me get you some coffee."

Colin held up his hand to stop him, but he did take a seat at the table.

"I'm actually on my way to go see Connor. If you don't mind, I will take some time and stay with you while I'm here. If it's too short of notice and you have other things going on, I can always stay up at the Turtledove Inn."

"You know you don't even have to ask," Nolan said.

After a few moments of silence and Kim slipping by and refilling his cup, Colin spoke. "How are you doing, Nolan?" Colin asked.

This was one of the things that Nolan really appreciated about Colin. Colin knew him. He knew what being here would mean to him. He knew the challenges that he was facing trying to do this job. But he wasn't ready to start that conversation yet.

"Are you here alone, Dad? I thought that you were hooking up with that lady next door, Margie Caswich?"

His dad held his hands out on the table and then shook his head. "Things didn't work out the way that I had hoped they would."

Nolan tried to remember something about Margie that he really liked, but to be truthful, he couldn't remember a thing. Margie was loud and outgoing, and his dad stayed home a lot; it didn't seem like that was the woman for him. On top of everything else, Nolan didn't think that his dad really got all that excited about the woman. Maybe it was different when you got older, but somehow, Nolan didn't think so.

"She was a good woman. You know, I just think that we weren't right for each other," his dad said. "Anyway, stop trying to change the subject. How long do you think you're going to be in this town?"

"I don't know. Things have taken a change that I didn't see coming."

"You spoke to the mayor, right? I mean, that's the norm how this goes. A big company comes into town; they see all of the administration, and then they make a decision."

"Well, I want to make sure that I give the town the best chance that it has, and the mayor is not the most straightforward person to deal with," Nolan hedged.

"I have faith that you can do this, Nolan. I know you enjoy the work that you do at Wealth Builders. You and Connor have become good friends, and I know that whatever your personal feelings are, you have never let them get in the way of business. When I first met you, I knew you were going to make something great of yourself."

It was that unwavering faith that made Nolan so grateful to have found his dad.

"So, let me bring up the elephant in the diner, so to speak. You know you're not that far from your mother?"

And in one sentence, all of his muscles tensed, his shoulders bunched, and his hands clenched around the coffee cup.

"I'm working," Nolan said. The answer sounded flimsy even to his ears. That was part of the other reason for the mounting of tension that was here. He was so close to his mother's town, and he knew it was rude not to at least see her for dinner. Nolan was waiting for the last moment as if he would be able to say he ran out of time.

If truth be told, it wasn't as if he was holding a grudge against his mother. He actually sent her gifts and made sure that she was taken care of wherever she decided to go. Colin had told him that a man always took care of his responsibilities. He didn't need to go to any therapist or psychologist to find the answer to the strain between them. He could accept that his mother, for whatever reason, had gotten herself into a bad situation, but Nolan thought children were beyond precious. More importantly, Nolan thought that if Colin could see there was something great in him worth fighting for, how come his own mother couldn't?

His dad reached across the table and placed his hands over his. "Take the time to see her, Nolan. It doesn't cost you a thing, and there may come a time when you don't have her here, and you'll regret the lost moments."

Nolan took a sip from his coffee cup so that he wouldn't have to answer. It also gave him a chance to regroup so he could try to find something politically correct to say to his father.

"Let me look into my schedule, Dad, and then I'll do what I can."

His dad didn't push him. Instead, he sat back in the booth and nodded to him.

"Well, listen, I've got to go to the inn, but I will see you later on."

Nolan nodded but didn't look him in the eye. Having his dad here was a plus and a minus. He was thrilled that his dad had finally decided to take some time off and come view the Turtledove Inn. He wanted somebody to make sure that he was doing things objectively, but he didn't want his dad to see that he was still so affected. When his dad stood up to leave, he patted him on the shoulder and then walked out of the diner.

Nolan watched him walk out of the diner and then looked back into his coffee cup. The situation was just becoming more and more complicated. Was it even worth it? He could write up his report now and save everybody the problems. He could save Layla from having to spend more time with him. He and his dad could leave early, and he wouldn't even have to worry about seeing his mother.

Yes, this was turning out to be just what he thought, a pain at the end of the day. That's what all small towns wound up being, anyway.

Colin walked out of the diner to his car. He didn't notice the beautiful day or the sun outside. His thoughts were already on the phone call he knew he had to make. After he got into his car, he pulled out his cell phone.

It was all so complicated, and it didn't have to be. Nolan was a man that any father would be proud of. Now that Nolan was older, maybe he would understand. Now that he was capable of having a family of his own, perhaps he would be able to forgive.

When he had gotten the call from Connor this morning, he knew something was wrong with Nolan. This something had been building for a while, and as he looked at his phone in his hand, he knew the answer wasn't going to be any easier now than it had been when Nolan was born.

Colin was stuck between a rock and a hard place. Maybe a better saying would be he was stuck between two of the most important people he had ever loved in his life. In order to save one, he might have to go ahead and hurt the other. He had made this decision once before, and the results hadn't been what either one of them thought it would be.

Time might heal all wounds, but it surely wasn't forgiving. It was time now to make things right, and stalling wasn't going to get him any closer to getting this together.

He opened up his cell phone and typed in Ellen's name. Of course, he had spoken to her on more than one occasion. They had been playing this game of saying they only spoke to one another just for the sake of Nolan, but that was another issue. He couldn't believe he was sitting in his car, hesitating to push a button in order to call this woman. He was no fresh boy out of college; he was a grown man. Yet, here he sat in his car, nervous as if it were the first date or prom night. He pushed the button and then put the call on speaker.

"Hello?"

Even her voice still gave him pause.

"Hello, is anyone on the line?"

"Ellen, it's me, Colin."

"Colin? Is Nolan ok?"

Well, that was the question of the day, wasn't it? That was why he was giving her a call. Nolan wasn't ok.

"Ellen, we need to talk. Nolan is in Inheritance Bay."

"Inheritance Bay? What is he doing there? That's just about fifteen to twenty minutes away from me."

"He's here for work."

"He didn't call me," she said in a small voice.

"Ellen, don't look into it. I think we need to talk about this."

"I think his actions are making it very clear. He's this close, and he doesn't even leave a message for me?"

"He just got here yesterday, and I knew that you were going to have this kind of reaction, so I wanted to talk to you beforehand so we could come up with a plan."

He heard nothing but silence.

"Business is why he's here. Coming up with a plan? There's nothing to plan. Really Colin, I just think—"

"We are going to have to tell him."

"No."

"Ellen, how long do you think we can go ahead and do this?"

"No, Colin. We are not going to tell him anything because I am the only one here with something to lose. He stays with you. He loves you. He adores you. He deals with me."

"Let's at least meet up and talk about it. I think that if you have some time to think and I have some time to think, when we get together, we can at least both agree on a final decision. At least give me that."

"Fine, but I don't think that anything is going to change."

"I don't have a date right now. Let me give you a call later on, ok. Can I call you, Ellen?"

"Yes, Colin, you can call me. I know we never seem to meet under the best circumstances, but I want you to know I missed you."

Colin hung up the phone, feeling encouraged and scared all at the same time. This time they were going to have to do the right thing. This time they were going to have to do what was best for their son and not for them.

Six

As soon as Layla walked into her store, she picked up her phone and sent an SOS out on her group chat. It took less than an hour, and all of them were there. The people she counted on in case of an emergency. The people she could call on when no one else was around.

Her brother sat next to Marjorie, the town organizer, and Poppy, the store manager. Layla and Ryan would be helpless without her. The last person to arrive—and when she did, she was harried—was Carrie, the doctor. Layla couldn't fault Carrie for coming in all flustered because it was hard being a doctor, teacher, and pharmacist in the small town.

After her mom had passed away, these were the people who had stood by her and helped her to go on. They had been her friend when she was growing up, and they had kept her mother's memory alive by telling her stories of times when her mother had first come to the town.

"I want to thank all of you for coming on such short notice."

"What's going on? Is there an emergency show that's coming up?" Poppy wanted to know. "Ryan wouldn't let me in on anything one way or the other."

"How can I let you know about something that I don't know anything about?" Ryan complained. "The only thing Layla told me was I needed to hurry up and get my butt over here, so we're all in the same boat."

"Well, I don't want to be the Debbie-downer here, but I hope that whatever is going on is extremely important because I had to go ahead and pull a substitute to watch a bunch of kids who are right now probably running amok in the class. As you can tell, the school is a little short-handed, and of course, I volunteered again for the science classes."

Layla took Carrie's complaining with a grain of salt. Everyone knew that she loved children. But only a few people knew that Carrie couldn't have any. Not wanting to delay the inevitable any longer, she cleared her throat and looked at Carrie.

"This won't take long. I know you are all in the midst of something."

"I'm fairly sure I know what this is about. It's about the cretin who moved in next door to you," Carrie said.

No one was surprised or even had to ask who she was talking about. Layla had to say that Nolan was correct on one mark: in a small town, news traveled fast.

"Shoot, I was hoping that it was going to be about you letting everyone know that you live here," Marjorie said despondently. Layla didn't even have to look at Ryan to know he was getting his hackles up.

"Well, if this meeting is about you sitting with Nolan in the diner, I think everybody already knows that already," Poppy said.

Layla turned to Poppy and looked at her incredulously.

"I just got back in the store. How could everybody know about me at the diner?"

Then everyone in the room answered in unison, "Blake."

Some days it took all of Layla's concentration not to be frustrated with the people she loved so much in this town.

"Ok, enough with the speculation, let's cut to the chase. Remember, there are a bunch of rebel children getting ready to storm a poor substitute teacher. Obviously, we're here because of Nolan. What is it that you'd like to say about it?" Carrie asked in her no-nonsense way.

"Yes, tell us all what he wants. So far, you're the only one besides the mayor that he's talked to. And we all know what it's like trying to talk to the mayor. One moment he says one thing, and if you say the wrong thing, he's switching 360 degrees," Ryan said, exasperated.

Layla was happy she didn't have a lot of emergencies in her life. Sometimes talking to all the people you loved at once was like herding kittens, and you were a mouse. They circled and circled, but none of them moved in any one direction.

"The following will be occurring. For reasons that I won't be explaining, I'll be spending a little extra time with Nolan while he's here—"

"Woohoo, it's Nolan, is it?" Poppy said slyly.

"What?" Ryan burst out.

Layla looked at all of the people in the room.

"Hear me. I need you all to be on your best behavior. Marjorie, do we have any events in Inheritance Bay going on or coming up? I need an update if you can give me one. I'd like Nolan to see what the Bay looks like in a festive light. Carrie, for a week, try not to argue with everyone about how overworked you are. Poppy and Ry, I'm going to need for you to do a shift or two of mine."

"Why?" Ryan pushed.

Layla turned and faced her brother. "Because I asked you to, and you trust me."

"Well, he came at a good time. I mean, we're about to celebrate the first day of spring," Marjorie said.

"That's true. A lot of people come here to see the new flowers and to get the latest pottery. It's going to be a great time for him to be here," Poppy chimed in.

Layla had completely forgotten that the first day of spring was coming. It looked like there wouldn't be a problem showing Nolan the best side of Inheritance Bay after all. Turning to Marjorie, she had an exciting feeling flow through her.

"Marjorie, can you get me a list of the activities for that day?" Layla asked.

"Of course."

Ryan grunted. "I don't think we should be going out of our way for this man, no matter what."

Layla reached out and touched her brother's arm. "I know you don't like this, and I want you to know that I appreciate your confidence in me. Hold tight with me, and it will all eventually make sense."

Everyone else was on board, but she knew going in that her brother would be a challenge.

"Trust me. I can handle Nolan Taggert."

Nolan had to seriously reconsider how crafty Layla was.

He thought her just a talented potter, but now he had to admit she had gotten the better of him in a way that most of his competitors would not believe. What made it worse was he had asked for this, and that meant she was crafty enough to make him complicit in his own downfall.

His dad had stayed at the Turtledove Inn yesterday. When his phone rang this morning, he thought it was him calling to ask for a ride or to meet for breakfast. Instead, it was Layla inviting him to try breakfast in a new place. He was more than willing to kill two birds with one stone. He'd listen to Layla talk about how great the Bay was, get a free meal, and he'd be able to sit with an attractive woman.

He had his game plan, and if it all went well, he'd be on his way home before the end of the week. Then he could leave this small town and go to a civilized city where no one knew his name, and how much he tipped was more important than where he was from.

When Nolan arrived at the store, he was met by a hostess who welcomed him to the Spring Festival planning session. The private interlude he thought he was about to have was filled with everyone from the town. At least it looked like everyone who owned a business in the town.

Layla was dressed in a flowing green dress and all smiles. Her cheeks had a bit of color in them, and everywhere she went, she managed to lightly touch everyone on the shoulder or in some way acknowledge them.

He had told her to keep the reason why he was here a secret. He was quite sure the mayor hadn't sold him out, either. He assumed that they were going to have several get-togethers or meetings alone so she could point out the better parts of town. He had been outwitted, but instead of him being upset, he was intrigued.

Being at this planning session was more intense than being at the diner, though. Everyone seemed to know their position at the individual tables. Every table had a different activity or was showcasing some parts of their business. When he walked by each table, everyone's speech became slow, as if they were trying to concentrate on two things at one time. Again, it came to him that being here in a small town meant everybody knew everyone's business. He didn't think that Layla had outed him, but she had definitely made him the center of attention.

He was trying to get to the smiling Layla in the middle of the room. She didn't try to move away. Instead, she stood there talking to people, almost as if she were daring him to approach her. Every time he made a step toward her, some person would try to interfere and ask his name. After the third person, he was beginning to become frustrated and wondered if he should just walk out now.

"I've seen that look before, and let me say, rethink whatever it is you were going to do."

"How do you show up in these places?" Nolan asked, shocked to see his dad.

"Riley brought me over with her today. She said there was a meeting in town and free breakfast. I figured I'd get some food, and then I'd meet you at the house. I'm surprised to see you here. Does this mean that you are having a change of heart?"

"No, not at all. I was pulled in by a crafty woman. I fell for the oldest trick in the book, a pretty face," Nolan said.

"I think you need to give her the benefit of the doubt."

"I think her tricking me here is all of the proof I need about her intentions," Nolan said.

His dad placed his hands on his shoulder. "Remember what she has at risk, Nolan. Do you blame her?"

Nolan wanted to respond, but then Layla rang a bell, and everyone stopped. It was like a weird game of musical chairs. Everywhere he looked, people sat. Then a woman came up behind his father. It was Riley with a smile on her face, and she gave him a nod as he walked his dad to a table where she sat. Then Layla walked up to him and slipped her arm into his.

She was all smiles, so Nolan pasted a smile on his face as he looked around. She guided him to the front of the room and gave him a seat at a round table in front of everyone. He couldn't believe her gall, and at the same time, he was impressed beyond measure that she had lured him here, and he hadn't even seen it coming. Nolan was so sure he knew what Layla was going to do, and then she surprised him.

Nolan could leave. He'd walked out of bigger meetings.

But when he looked at Layla, standing triumphantly at the front of the room, he took his seat and gave her her due. On another woman, the green dress might have made their skin look sallow and sickly. On Layla, the green dress gave her a glow like some nymph walking amongst the mortals. With rosy cheeks and a glint of mischief in her eyes, she looked as though she was in her element.

"Good morning, everyone. I'm so glad that you could all make it. As you know, in two days, we will celebrate the first day of spring. I know that each one of you has been making preparations individually, but Marjorie has decided this year that we should get together and put the fair booths on Main Street. That way we can keep all of the visitors in one place. Normally, Clay Works doesn't advertise due to our personal situation, but this year we are going to make an exception.

"Just so everybody will know, Marjorie has sent out several letters to past residents of Inheritance Bay. It is Marjorie's hope that by having these festivals, the prior residents will see the potential in our town and want to stay. I am a great believer in everyone in this town and what they do, and I believe that the skills and crafts that the Bay area offers are unique enough for everyone to find a path to prosperity. It's all about exposure, and that's what these festivals are about."

All at once, Nolan felt as though he had prejudged Layla incorrectly. His father had told him to be patient and not to judge too soon. So that's how she came to be at this morning's breakfast. It wasn't that she was trying to trick him—it was that Marjorie was trying to get more people to want to stay in the Bay. He could understand the technique. If anything, it worked with Riley, and now she was running the Turtledove Inn.

"Now, we've decided to bribe you all here by offering breakfast, but Marjorie will be coming around to every table. She will have a clipboard, and I'll need you to let her know what you're going to be selling, what your specialty is, and where you would like your booth to be set up on Main Street. If we all work together, this will be the best Spring Festival ever at Inheritance Bay. Thank you. Now eat up, and don't forget to give her your information when she comes by."

"Layla, before you sit down," Marjorie said quickly. "We all want to know. Who's the new guy at your table? Will he be staying for the festival?"

Layla looked surprised. Her smile was a little tighter than he had seen before. With the practice that came with experience, he stood up and looked toward Marjorie. Marjorie was an older woman, and he had to make sure that his response was concise and respectful.

"I haven't decided what my plans are going to be. What I will say is that Layla has been kind enough to show me around and if my schedule permits, I would look forward to seeing all that Inheritance Bay has to offer."

He took his seat, and everyone seemed to calm down after that. He wasn't really concerned about what anyone else thought. His focus was on Layla and how she had gotten the better of him. Nolan was laughing at himself and looking forward to his interaction with her.

Layla sat next to him and leaned over. "In case I don't get a chance to say it later, thank you for not walking out."

He wondered if she knew that there were some strands

of her hair that were brushing his shoulder. She was leaning toward him to keep her words just between them, but all he could focus on was her soft scent and errant strands that landed on his shoulder and brushed against him. There was an urge to reach out and touch the strands to see if they were as soft as he thought.

"What kind of man would walk out on a beautiful woman?"

"Well, it's happened, so don't think you'd be the first one," she quipped back.

"That just goes to show you the problem with small towns. They don't know a treasure when they see one," he said.

Layla gave him a smirk. "I've been called a lot of things but never a treasure. Let's just say I have a way of saying what is on my mind, and most of the time, it's not what is popular."

He gave her a second look and really wanted to ask who had said that to her. Nolan appreciated Layla's forthrightness. In a world where people often didn't tell him the truth, she was a pleasant surprise. Nolan had heard bits and pieces of Layla's story. It was odd, but he felt as though he and Layla shared a history with coming to a small town. He wondered what her small-town experience had been like. He wondered how she could want to defend a small town after coming here as a stranger.

"People rarely want to hear the truth Layla," he said sympathetically.

"Maybe, but I'm still going to deliver it. I think bad things can happen, but the trick is to not let them change me."

It was a noble thought, and he wondered how long she would be able to maintain herself and not be changed by her surroundings. As Nolan thought about it, he was actually a little bit jealous. He had definitely been changed and shaped by his surroundings.

"So, if your little speech is correct, Clay Works will be on Main Street, is that right?"

"It is. It's not something I would have chosen to do, but I do feel like I'm obligated to do it to help out the Bay."

"No one can force you to do that. You know that, right?"

"You make it seem like they are holding me hostage, but the fact is I could have said no to Marjorie."

"Why didn't you?" he asked.

Layla shrugged. "How could I say no and still look everyone in the eye? I have an obligation to help everyone since I'm a part of the community. That's what community means, helping out when you can and being there for your neighbors."

He looked at her and could see no trace of insincerity, and still, he was fascinated. He knew his past was getting in the way, but there was a part of him that thought no one who had come to a small town and had to be accepted could be that happy with the whole experience. Small towns were insular and treated all foreigners as potential threats initially.

"I wonder if you would think this if someone sold your location to a local paper?" He could tell his tone had been harsh when Layla pulled away.

"Really? Is that what you think would happen?"

"I think people are people."

Layla gathered his plate and then stood up. "I feel bad if those are the only people you have known. But my mother would say you have brought that behavior on to yourself."

"What?"

"My mom would say that the first thing you suspect others of would be the first thing you'd do yourself in that same situation. Just think about that."

Nolan watched her walk away with his plate and wondered if there was any truth to her statement.

Seven

Breakfast had been a disaster. Layla didn't know what she was thinking by inviting Nolan. What she was really upset about was that Nolan accused the people of Inheritance Bay of doing things that he would do himself. Who did that?

It was lunchtime, and she was still going over the catastrophe of breakfast. What was it about him that just made her forget all of her etiquette? Tricking people to go to events under false pretenses was definitely not a polite move. She knew why he was here. Layla understood that a lot was riding on what happened between her and Nolan.

There was something about this man that made her say whatever was on her mind. It was like he was her personal antagonist. Nolan knew how to get under her skin without even trying. She had gathered together her emergency group to help her out so that she could take some time in being nice to Nolan and showing him around Inheritance Bay.

Why was she having such a hard time doing this? As

she walked in through the front door of her store, she saw Poppy standing there trying to wave at her in a short, odd way.

"Poppy, I don't know what it is, but I'm just not as focused as I need to be. I think I'm going to go to my office." Layla said the words, and as she did, Poppy's face fell. It wasn't until she was standing next to her that she understood the reason. Standing not even three feet behind Poppy, leaning against the counter in her store, was Nolan Taggert.

"I'm glad you're on your way to the office. That way, I won't have to make an appointment. I'll just follow you."

If it had been possible, Layla would have just fallen into the ground and let the whole earth swallow her up. How did this man just show up, and why couldn't she escape him?

"Follow me, since you are already here," she said, trying not to let the exhaustion and hopelessness of the situation filter through her voice.

Layla walked to the back, and Nolan followed her. When she unlocked the office, he went in and took a seat right away. If there were going to be a fight, then she would start it and finish it.

"So, the first day of spring is a big deal, and it will attract a lot of tourist money. If you had your call center here, they would benefit from being on-site because, in this town, there is not just their work but relaxation."

"I suppose it must be a lot of money for a small town," he replied. "The call center employees would be coming from larger cities most likely, as well as recruited from the local area. The first day of spring isn't a federal holiday. While it might be busy for you, it would be a regular day for others."

"You're right. The first day of spring is busy for us. You might find that the celebration is unique and has a bigger draw than you originally thought. Anyway, you'll be able to weigh in as we go through the events."

"Go through the events?" Nolan asked.

"You hadn't appeared to be this slow when we first met."

She watched Nolan raise an eyebrow and give her a look of disbelief.

"You will be here. We will go through the events, and you'll see what the appeal is of the festival. Certainly, you could tell from the breakfast that everyone wants you to attend the Spring Festival."

"I thought we had an agreement. Why do they even care what I do either way?"

Layla rolled her eyes and tried to keep her cool. "You know I don't think you have a lot of friends. At first, I thought it was because you're this type-A personality that is always working. Now I know it's because you believe you are the smartest person on the planet, and no one else has any real thoughts. I don't need to tell anyone anything about you. You're an executive of Wealth Builders. You're not staying with Conner at the inn, and you're walking around town. Everyone wants to know what you are doing here, and since you're not talking to the locals, everyone wants to see where you go and what you do. Remember, you and Conner are unknown."

"Conner is here with Riley," Nolan shot back.

"He's with Riley now, but he didn't start that way," Layla replied.

"What is it that they think Connor and I are actually going to do in this small town?"

Layla could feel the smile coming over her face. There it was again, that mischievous feeling that this man just inspired in her. "I don't know. To be honest, no one knows what you and Connor want to do here in Inheritance Bay. For all anyone knows, you could decide to open up a casino."

Nolan laughed out loud. "Can you imagine how much it would cost to get people to come out here?"

Layla gave him a skeptical look. "So, you're saying it's a definite no on the casino, huh?"

Nolan looked at her and then shook his head. He let out a big sigh and then relaxed into the chair he was sitting in.

"Let me be the first one to tell you that Connor came here just to make his parents happy. He was supposed to leave after that was over. It was only because he met, and fell in love with, Riley that he's even still here in this small town."

"Is that a note of derision that I hear in your voice?"

"It's not derision that you hear. It's just a weird twist of fate that he wound up staying here."

"Certainly, you have to admit, Nolan, that if Connor can find someone and something here, that must indicate that Inheritance Bay can't be all bad."

"I didn't say that Inheritance Bay was bad."

"That's right, you didn't say that, but what you did do was lump Inheritance Bay in with every other small town you have ever seen. You need to be able to look at the Bay area on its own merits. I don't know what it is you said to the mayor, but I don't think you can really do that. I would be shocked if you could even stay during the Spring Festival and enjoy any of the events. Your bias seems deep-rooted, and it's going to stop the people of the Bay from getting a fair shot."

Layla looked at Nolan's face as it tightened under the strain of her words. Why couldn't she for once just go along with whatever it was everybody else was saying? Just when she was trying to formulate some kind of apology, Nolan let out a sigh and then said words she never thought she'd hear him say.

"You're right."

Layla sat back in her chair and let out a sigh. "My goodness, it's about time you recognized that I was right. Since you were already on the right track, let me also let you know that you're going to have a great time at the Spring Festival."

Nolan laughed. "You never give up, do you?"

"Of course, I do. I always make sure to give up when I'm wrong." Layla knew she was pushing the envelope, but still, she couldn't stop herself. "So now that we've decided that I'm right and you're going to have a great time at the festival, I'll come by and pick you up and be your escort."

Nolan stood and gave her a second look.

"This is the first time a woman has said she's going to come by and pick me up."

"Don't get used to it, Nolan; it took a Spring Festival for me even to ask you out. Think of this as our first and only date."

"We will see."

With those words, Nolan walked out of her office,

leaving Layla strangely out of breath. She was going to have to show him the Spring Festival, and then after that, Layla was going to spend an awful lot of time with her pottery and her clay. When she needed to clear her mind, she always went to her art, and Nolan was the kind of man you needed to clear out of your mind.

Nolan was sitting in the backyard, and he was overcome by a sense of peace he hadn't felt in a long time. He was in no rush to go anywhere, and he had no meetings to prepare for. He imagined if he lived in the Bay, this would be the norm. Standing in the backyard, looking up at the stars and soaking up the quiet moments in life. Hearing the cicadas' rhythm and absorbing the cool breeze that came off of the Bay and brought with it a caress and took away any worries from the day.

This was what it was like to live on a postcard. Although to be fair, Nolan knew it was more than that. Nolan had traveled the world and been on more beaches than he had been in apartments. One of the perks of working at Wealth Builders was that he was able to travel the world. Yes, somehow, even though he had been everywhere, being here in the backyard under the starry sky seemed to be the most peaceful place he had ever been on the planet.

It was quiet nights like this when he and his father had sat in another backyard. Colin had taken an angry foster child and taught him how to contain his anger and focus.

Nolan didn't want to think of why he had been angry as a child. As quickly as the memory had come, he pushed it away and stood up out of the chaise lounge he had been sitting in.

The sun was setting, and just like clockwork, Layla was coming home. He didn't have to wonder if it was her. Layla took her little charge out in a basket every evening. He hadn't gotten a chance to really see the dog, but he knew about the dog in the basket. He got a glimpse of the dog on the first day, but truth be told, Nolan had spent his time looking at Layla and not the animal.

What he did know was that the dog's name was Princess. And Layla would talk to this dog all of the time. She would tell her how pretty she was and how brave she was. Listening to her encourage this little dog made Nolan reevaluate all the other women he had ever dated. How many of those women would have been caught with such a little dog in a basket, toting it around, much less constantly encouraging it. Layla was a rare find.

When Nolan saw Layla coming in through the back, he should have turned around and gone back to his house. He should have ignored her and then waited ten or fifteen minutes and then come back out. But there was something about Layla that made him ignore logic and the sensible thing to do. So instead of ignoring his neighbor and going back in, he did what every neighborly person did; he called out to her.

"Hello there."

She hadn't been expecting anyone to say anything and her first instinct was to tighten her grip on the basket where the dog was. When she realized who it was, she let out a sigh.

"Oh, it's you. Hi."

"Don't sound so enthused. You know I see you carrying this dog everywhere. You want to tell me why?"

"Honestly, I don't want to tell you, but somehow, I don't think you're going to let me get away with that."

"You're right. So what gives?"

"I foster rescues. Princess was rescued from a puppy mill, and she doesn't quite know how to walk on solid ground. She's only been in a cage most of her life, so until she gets on her feet, I don't mind toting her around a little bit."

"Do you have plans for dinner?"

Layla raised her eyebrow and made sure that her basket was a little higher on her shoulder. "Are you inviting me over for dinner?"

"I'm suggesting that if you're free and I'm free, there's no sense we shouldn't be together, that's all."

"Fine, let me go put Princess up, and I'll be right over."

As Layla went into her home, Nolan had to ask himself what he was doing. He always planned everything, but when he was around Layla, he was playing it by ear. There was something so freeing about living on the fly. Layla made him remember what it was like not to live a completely planned life. Nolan would admit that he was focused on trying to make sure he made his father proud. After he had already accomplished his goal at Wealth Builders, maintaining the structure was second nature to him and was becoming boring.

Layla reminded him of the man he had been when he measured success in terms of family and people, not money.

Eight

Here Layla was, acting all out of character again. It was all because of that man, Nolan. She wasn't going to drive herself crazy, he had invited her to dinner, and she would just throw on whatever she found. After tossing four dresses to the side and then running into the shower, Layla had to face it: She was not just getting ready to see a friend. Nolan Taggert had asked her out on a date.

Technically it wasn't a real date because they weren't going out in public. They were just going to be good neighbors to one another and share a meal. No, she couldn't get her stomach to believe that and stop the butterflies that were flying around in circles. Maybe she could stop the heat from coloring her cheeks.

Layla jumped into the shower, and as the water sluiced over her, she thought it would be the perfect excuse for why she had so much color in her cheeks. It was obviously the result of the quick shower she had taken. She thought about the dress that was on her bed, and she knew she was going to wear it. She had been saving money for this dress for special occasions. Not that this was a special occasion, but in such a small town, when would she actually get to wear the dress? It was a long, white dress with blue butterflies on it, and Layla adored it.

Ten minutes later, she was out of the shower and smoothing the dress over her hips. She could do this. At the end of the day, Nolan was just another man. Her brother would laugh at her to see how she was so turned inside out. Ok, maybe he wouldn't laugh because right now, he didn't like Nolan at all.

When she walked into the backyard, Nolan stopped. "Layla?"

"Ok, ok, I can see that maybe this was too much for you."

"No, no, I'm happy that you dressed for dinner."

"It's not like it's formalwear. It's just a maxi dress. What are you trying to say, Nolan, that normally I don't look well put together?"

Nolan smiled. "Layla, you're going to have to explain that one to me. I can always tell when I'm talking about something that makes you uncomfortable; your first thing to try is to start a fight."

She was about to argue that fact, but she caught herself. As if Nolan could read her mind, he smiled at her, as well.

"I confess it's my go-to weapon, especially when it comes to men."

"Sorry," Nolan said. It was odd that she thought he was serious.

"Personal relationships are hard for me. It's one of the reasons why family means so much to me. It's one of the reasons why the people here in the Bay mean so much to me." Layla wanted to take back the last two minutes of that conversation. Was she telling this man absolutely everything about her after just meeting him? This was Nolan. The man who had come to decide whether or not her town was going to be able to survive.

Her mother always told her that to solve every problem was to acknowledge the problem. Nolan Taggert was an attractive man. She hadn't really forgiven him for being attractive, a nerd, and having money. It just seemed as though the deck was stacked against most women when it came to Nolan. OK, now that she had gotten that out of her system, she was going to be able to enjoy a normal dinner with Nolan for the rest of the night.

All she needed to do was concentrate on something else. She had to admit, he had cleaned up the backyard pretty well. There was a rectangular table covered with a red and white checkered cloth. On the table, he had already laid out some plates, some silverware, and two glasses. The sound of the evening crickets and cicadas greeted her as she took a seat. Without even mentioning her horrible confession, Nolan went to the grill to start the steaks.

Ok, maybe Nolan going to the grill wasn't the best thing for him to do because it was definitely a great view for Layla. She closed her eyes and took a deep breath. She could act her age and not her shoe size. What this experience was teaching her was that she needed to spend more time with people and maybe less time with her clay.

Finally, he turned around with the steaks on a plate. Was it her imagination, or had he hesitated and looked a little longer at her? Did he notice the dress that she had put on for tonight? She had to clear her mind and think about the steak, which looked amazing. Was there nothing that Nolan couldn't do?

"I invited you to dinner and didn't even ask you if you ate meat or if you wanted steak," Nolan said as he placed the plate on the table.

"No, I eat meat. I eat everything just fine, thanks."

If only she could sink into the ground, that would be merciful. Did she just say that she inhaled all things? Well, it was too late to take it back now.

"If you want, I think I have a bag of salad in the house," Nolan said.

"No, it's fine. I'm not really big on eating salads anyway. Well, now, since I've already made a big confession of mine already, it's time for you to share, Nolan. You are a closed book. Why don't you tell me something about Nolan Taggert?"

"I don't think there's really that much to tell. I was a foster child, and I was fortunate enough to be fostered and adopted by the same man. My father invested a lot in me and had a lot of faith in me. Then one day, I went to college and met Connor. After that is history."

"It's funny, I didn't grow up as a foster child, but my mom came here with my brother and me to Inheritance Bay. We had no family, and she never spoke of our family or where she came from. When we asked, she always told us that the only family we needed was here at the Bay. The town embraced my brother and me. So, it wasn't like we had a foster parent, but I would say everyone in this town probably had a hand in raising us."

She saw him tense up, and then Nolan served out the

steaks. She wasn't sure what had changed, but something had.

"Hey, did I miss something? It seems like we were talking, and then the whole vibe changed."

"I'm sorry. It's not you. My mother lived in a small town, too. I shouldn't say that—I should say, my mother lives in a small town not that far from here. It's called Sunset Valley."

"Yeah, I know where the Valley is. I go there sometimes. They are a little bit bigger than we are, but my understanding is they started out the same way Inheritance Bay did."

"Well, what you probably don't know is my mother is from there, and she had me when she was incredibly young, and times were different. So, the town there didn't embrace me, and they wouldn't have embraced her."

"Ah, I can see how you had a different experience. I'm sorry for that, Nolan. The only thing I can say to that is not every town is the same."

Listening to his experience, it was a wonder that he had even come to Inheritance Bay. She couldn't imagine living the life that Nolan had lived. But now, it made so much more sense why he seemed to have so much disbelief in the goodness of people. Originally, she had thought that Nolan's coldness had something to do with him being a businessperson. Now she knew that Nolan's attitude had more to do with how he was raised.

According to the gossip mill, there had been a man who sat down with Nolan in the diner. Layla was of the opinion that that man would probably be her ticket to getting to know Nolan.

"We all have our own dark mountains to climb, right?" Nolan said.

Layla nodded, but internally she thought there were some dark mountains that you climbed, and it was over, and others you just looked at, and they served as a barrier in your life.

"Give me a minute. I'm going to go and get us something to drink, and then I'll be right out."

When he came out of his house, he actually had a tray of items. There was a pitcher of iced tea, two cans of soda, and a small platter of dipping sauces for the steaks.

The evening went off without a hitch. It was actually one of the most enjoyable dates that she had had in an awfully long time. During the table conversation, she found Nolan to be knowledgeable on lots of different subjects. She would have thought as rich as he was and as focused as he seemed that the only thing he knew about was finance, but she was mistaken.

He spoke to her about animals, his travels to different continents to see national monuments, and spoke of his love of visiting castles on different continents. The man who had seemed like the grim reaper now seemed like a nice human being. After the plates were cleared away and they were both sitting in chaise lounges looking up at the stars, the questions turned toward her.

"Ok, I have been rambling on all night long. I feel like I've been giving you a dossier about my whole life. It's time for you to talk," he said. "The burning question that everybody wants to know is why you are still here in Inheritance Bay?"

She smiled and then sat up in the chair and looked over at him. He copied her movement so that they were facing each other knees to knees.

"I think it's a little bit arrogant of you to think I haven't seen the world," Layla said.

"Have you?"

"Yes, I have seen the world. I didn't start out with a degree in being a potter. I actually started out with a degree in mathematics. I went on to get my master's in education, and I left Inheritance Bay to go work in a research firm for a couple of years."

"Really?"

"I know it will come as a complete shock to you, but even though my mom came here and the town adores me, they still gave me the space to discover myself. I bet you thought that this is all I had ever seen, and that could be the only reason I would ever stay in Inheritance Bay?"

"I couldn't say that this is all you had ever seen, but I definitely wouldn't have said that you had ever had a job outside of the Bay for any long period of time."

"Well, I did. I was a woman at a great research firm moving up the corporate ladder. At the end of the day, what really happened was I started to burn out. Burnout in a research firm can happen anywhere from six to eight months. The thing that saved me was pottery. So, I started doing it on the side and going to little farmer's markets, and before long, it seemed as though a lot of people noticed what I was doing, and they liked it."

"So, when you were at the research firm, you lived in the city, right?"

"Yes, I did."

"Then help me out. Even after the burnout, you would have still had your apartment. Why not stay there?"

"The short answer is family. My brother, Ryan, had been taking care of our mother, and she was getting sicker, and I had to make some decisions. I was visiting home, of course, but I wanted to be there for her and for Ryan. It turned out that when I got here, Ryan wasn't doing pottery, but he was painting, and he was drawing, and so it became a natural progression for the both of us to teach each other our art forms, and then we came up with these new creations."

"You gave up your life and everything in the city for your family?"

Layla smiled at him and nodded. "I did, and I have to tell you something; there is not one day that I ever regret it. Now, my mom being my mom, what she hadn't told me was that she was a part of a shelter rescue program."

"Oh, and now that explains why you have Princess. I see that you are very dedicated to her. Are you planning on keeping her?"

"I'm actually not sure. Princess is never going to stop anyone from coming into my home. But there is something very comforting about me having to take care of her and her being with me all the time."

"And you're happy?"

Layla tried to hold back the aggravated sigh. "You mean, am I happy being in this small town with just my pottery, having to deal with the same people day in and day out and running my own store?"

"I'm sorry if I'm making it sound like that's a small feat. I guarantee you that I understand more than most what it takes to start a business and keep it afloat even when you are talented. Sometimes talent isn't enough. My question was, are you happy where you are right now?"

Layla listened to his words and then took a deep breath and let it out.

"I am happy now. There was a time when I got up every morning and went to a job, wasn't sure if I liked it, came back, and sat in my living room in the dark and wondered what I was doing with my life. I don't wonder anymore. I'm happy with the people who are in my life, and I'm happy with the way my life is going."

Nolan nodded. "Most people would say you have already gotten the American dream then."

It was on the tip of Layla's tongue to say, *But what about you?* The evening had gone so well that she didn't want to ruin it by pushing too much. But she had to admit that her curiosity was piqued by the very idea that this man who was rich beyond measure still seemed like he was searching and unhappy.

"Well, the American dream requires me to get myself up and go to work in the morning."

She thought she saw him about to hesitate and maybe offer her something else. Layla couldn't be sure that's what Nolan was going to do, but she thought she had picked the right dress when he stood up and held out his hand to hers.

She looked at the outstretched hand, and for a moment, she thought about not taking it. They were already so close that if she put her hands in his, they would definitely be in each other's personal space. Not wanting to be rude, she placed her hand in his, and he pulled her up to her feet.

Sure enough, he had pulled her right into his arms. He tried to back up, but his legs hit the chaise lounge, which also hit the little table next to it, and tilted it, knocking his glass over. He didn't even turn around; he just hung his head and let out a sigh.

"Tell me it's not the huge mess that I think it is behind me," he said in a low voice filled with embarrassment.

Layla looked around him to see what had transpired. When she took her other hand and tapped him on the shoulder so that his head lifted up, he looked her in the eyes.

"The good news is no one was hurt in the catastrophe. But I have to admit it does look impressive. It was a life-sized domino trick. You're in luck. I can help you clear that up in no time at all and clear off the table."

Nolan shook his head. "I clean up my own messes, but thank you. I want to thank you for coming tonight."

There was nothing super intimate about the words. But when he said them as they were standing so close to each other, they seemed to take on a whole new meaning. An errant breeze went through the backyard, and with it brought her the smell of clean soap. It was then that her unruly hair fell to her shoulders. Not all of it, just those strands that would never stay in their place. And as the wind blew through the backyard, those pieces traveled until they lightly grazed Nolan's face.

She opened her mouth to say to him that she was sorry. Reflexively she reached out to wet her lips, and when she looked up, she saw Nolan transfixed. They were so close it would take nothing for him to kiss her. If he just moved a centimeter or pulled her closer, that would definitely start it. He didn't move at all, and he didn't move her closer, either. But her hand that rested on his shoulder could feel the bunching of his muscles as if he was holding himself back.

Ok, this was when she had to remember she was attracted to this man and maybe he was attracted to her. She was the absolute worst person to be attracted to. But like her mother used to say, *When things happen, they happen for a reason, and most of the time, they're not convenient.*

She cleared her throat, tapped his shoulders, and then gave him a wide smile.

"Dinner was great. Next time I'll do the cooking."

He hadn't really let her go, and his eyes were still fixed on her lips, but then he nodded and gazed into her eyes. "Next time?"

She nodded. "Yes, next time. Besides, it's nothing personal; it's me just being neighborly. In case I didn't say this to you before, welcome to Inheritance Bay."

Nine

Nolan always believed in telling himself the truth. He could go into a business meeting and bluff the competition, or he could go into a social setting and bluff there. Nolan's Golden Rule was that you could say anything to anyone else, but you always had to tell yourself the truth.

The truth was, Nolan was in trouble.

As he stood in his kitchen cleaning up the dishes from that night's dinner, he couldn't help but remember standing close to Layla. What was it about this woman that made her so attractive? She wasn't the most beautiful woman he had ever met. In truth, the most attractive thing about Layla was her wit. She was a small fireball package of wit and courage. He might not agree with her that small towns were good, but he could tell she felt strongly about it.

Nolan just couldn't believe he had almost kissed her. More importantly, what was really playing in the back of his head was, if he had leaned down to kiss her, would she have allowed it? Layla was the full package, and because she was a woman that men look forward to marrying, that made her off-limits to him. Kissing a beautiful woman under the moonlight was one thing, but Layla was the kind of woman you married.

He was in town to do a job. He wasn't in town to romance the locals. No matter how great it felt between them, Nolan had to keep his focus. It was because he kept his focus on his career that he had even gotten this far. Marriage and family were words that came to him when he thought about stepping down and retiring. Getting married was something people did when they weren't on the hunt or when men weren't in their prime. Remembering his own life as a child didn't entice him to be married or a parent.

He thought about Connor and Riley and how it had worked out for them. He sincerely hoped that they made it. Connor had changed and had become less focused on work and more focused on Riley. What was more important was that when Connor and Riley were together, they were happy, and they looked as though they had found the missing pieces of themselves.

While Nolan looked at the couple and thought they had finally found the right way to make it work, Nolan wasn't so sure there was such a path for him. He had everything he could want. He had several houses, and he had a career he loved. True, he wasn't with any particular woman, but if he wanted to go out on a date, there were several he could call up, and they would be more than happy to go out with him.

Despite what he may have thought about his mother, he always took care of her. His father would never let him forget that no matter how he felt about her, a good man takes care of his mother. He checked in on her and sent her gifts and cash, although she always tried to return them. Nolan had to admit that the most important person in his life was Colin. His dad had stood by him through school and was even the reason he joined the startup. He had never once wavered in his faith in him. Even his father had decided to go on dates.

As he was finishing up the dishes and he hung the dish rag on the underside of the sink, he wondered. Was he really content? Being content and getting married were not the same thing. But what he could say was Layla made him think about that. When he thought about being in a relationship with a woman or even when he was looking for someone compatible, never in a million years would he have looked in a small town.

Layla's words came back to him and echoed in his mind. When she said, she used to come home and sit in the dark. He didn't want to tell her he had done the same thing. Nolan shook his head and tried to put these things out of his mind. He wasn't in Inheritance Bay to reevaluate his life. He wasn't in Inheritance Bay to find the woman of his dreams. He was here to do a job, which was to evaluate a small town. In order to make sure he stayed focused, he had to make a resolution that he was not going to let Layla get under his skin. Dinner tonight had been a slip but a valuable lesson. He would keep everything about the business, make his decision and then leave the town. He had taken on corporations. He could certainly handle Layla.

It was the first day of the two-day Spring Festival. Layla was trying to find a way to get Inheritance Bay underneath Nolan's skin. As she walked through the lane, she had never seen so many visitors come for the festival. As she looked about and saw the fruits of everyone's labor being appreciated by so many, she couldn't help but be proud of her town and the people in it.

She had to admit that she was a little nervous about the turnout for the festival. Nolan was here to see that Inheritance Bay was a good place to set up shop, and if there weren't enough people, she figured that would be one more hurdle she'd have to get over. However, seeing all of these people here, she hoped that it would show Nolan that moving his center here would be a great idea.

It wasn't just that there was a festival going on but that every group was represented during the festival. There were events for children and events for adults. At the end of both sides of Main Street and the lane, there was a band setting up. On the right-hand side, it was classical music, and on the left, it was jazz.

Her brother had finally made it to the festival and their booth. When he arrived, she took the opportunity to walk up and down Main Street to see how the booths were going and if anyone else needed any help.

"Hello, Layla," Serenity called out. "This Spring Festival is so busy. Thanks for helping us set up!"

They were sitting in their booth called Two Sticks and a Thread, but the town called them Silver Fox sisters. One of them was Tara, and the other one was called Serenity. She had never met two sisters who could be more different. They were only separated by two years, but it could have been forever. Tara was always dressed in dark blue. She wore dresses that came down to her ankles and covered her arms down to her wrists. Serenity, on the other hand, looked as though she had been a flower child. All of her dresses were brightly colored, and most of the time, they looked as though they had been hand tie-dyed. The only thing the sisters seemed to agree on was hairstyle and hair color. Their hair was always nicely curled with a highlight of purple on their silver heads. At the age of sixty-five, they were still mobile, and they still ran their store, Two Sticks and a Thread.

"It's no problem, Serenity. I'm always here to help." Layla smiled and kept on walking. At the end of the day, what she had told Serenity was the truth. One of the things she loved about being in Inheritance Bay was that everybody was there to help everybody.

Layla looked at each booth as if she had seen it for the first time. When she finally got to the end of the lane, she found some bleachers, and sitting in them was Nolan, surrounded by some vendors and shop owners from Inheritance Bay. She could see him nodding his head as if he were really paying attention. But every so often, she saw his eyes scan the crowd until they landed on her. He looked as though he was about to stand up, but when he did, someone else tried to catch his attention.

Layla took this opportunity to turn and go in the opposite direction. She really needed to get a grip on what was going on here. The town had to come before her. And the truth of the matter was that if last night showed her anything, it was that the attraction to Nolan was stronger than she initially thought. She couldn't believe how much that almost kiss had been on her mind. If they had actually kissed, where would she be then? Just the thought of how close she was in his arms, close enough with her hands on his shoulders to feel the blood flow beneath her fingertips. Even when she recalled the moment, she got a slight hitch in her breath and her eyes closed as if somehow, by closing them, she could relive the almost moment.

At the time, she hadn't been sure, but now she had firmly convinced herself that he was disappointed that he hadn't kissed her, either. That hesitation before bending down, the tensing underneath her hands—yep, she was sure he had wanted to kiss her. Then her reverie was broken by a voice she could have lived without hearing for today.

"I'm surprised you're not in your own stall selling your wares, Layla."

Layla took a deep breath before she turned around so that she could put on a smile and try to get through dealing with Micah Hamilton.

"I was there, but Ryan came to help me out, so I decided to look at everybody else's stuff."

Micah considered himself to be her competition in town. Layla didn't even see him that way. In the beginning, when Layla had come back home, she had taken her work and put it in the consignment shop. Micah Hamilton ran the consignment shop, and everybody brought in their crafts and goods to him so that he could go ahead and sell them.

The first year Layla came, she gave all her goods to Micah, and he sold them. The problem was that Micah had contracted to give her a certain percentage of the set price. She found out he had raised the prices but hadn't raised her percentage share, and that had been her impetus to leave. So, after two years, Layla made a decision. She would no longer send her goods to Micah, but she would sell them on her own in her own shop.

After Layla left Micah, many other vendors decided to try to sell their own items, too, or partnered up and opened their own stores. Micah always said that her leaving was the reason his store could only be open two or three days out of the week. There just wasn't enough product and wasn't enough demand to come to his store.

"You know that's one of the things you always have to watch. You think that you're on top one day, and all of your sales are going good, but then before you know it, the rug is pulled right from underneath you."

Layla smiled. "I think you are absolutely right, and that's why I am so grateful to have Ryan."

Micah sniffed and then looked around the festival. "Weren't you on the committee that put this festival together?"

"Yes." Layla braced herself for whatever new round of criticism Micah was about to deliver.

"It just seems to me that if the committee wanted to make sure this was a big success, they would've asked Connor to come down."

"I think today is a big success for us all, Micah. It's true, Connor could have come down and added some more star power to the event, but I think it's just as important that we're able to attract people without having to use any of that power."

"Of course, Layla, I was just trying to be helpful."

No matter what she did, Micah would not be happy. Had she invited Connor, he would have said that she was desecrating the festival by inviting outsiders. She hadn't invited Connor, and now she was shortchanging the neighborhood. Layla understood she just couldn't win when it came to Micah.

"I want to thank you so much, Micah, for offering that help. It takes all of us in the Bay to make festivals work."

Micah snorted. "You know, I never know how sincere you really are, Layla. I hope, though, that you are sincere about doing what's best for the Bay."

"Of course."

Then Micah took a step closer to Layla, as if he was whispering something in her ear. "So, are you going to tell me what Nolan is doing here in town?"

"What Nolan is doing?"

"Yes, you know, people like him don't just show up in small towns for no reason. There's got to be something going on. He lives right next door to you, so if anybody knows, it would be you. What plans does Nolan have for Inheritance Bay? I mean, we all heard the speech that Connor gave, but I think we can all agree that speech was made because Riley told him to do it."

It was moments like these that Layla wanted to turn around and announce that Nolan was here to evaluate the town and everybody had to fall in line. But she had given her word, and she wouldn't break it now. At the end of the day, telling Micah might not be as helpful as she'd like to think.

"If you have any questions, Micah, I think you should take those up with Nolan."

"You're probably right. I mean, why would he even bother telling you? He would probably want to talk to someone important like the mayor, you know, or even me. So many people come to my shop, and I'm the focal point. Before everyone starts being so nice to Nolan, we should make sure we know his intentions."

"This is a town, Micah. We don't need to know everyone's intentions. We just need to get along."

"You say that now, but let me tell you, knowing a person's intentions is very important if you want to stay ahead of them."

She wanted to understand Micah and his mentality to hunt down all things new and find out if they are going to disrupt the peace. It didn't help that there was a grain of truth in what Micah was saying. She looked at the people on the land, and then she thought about some other parts of town that were empty and needed to be rented. All of a sudden, the task of showing Nolan the best time was starting to feel insurmountable. She took a deep breath and tried to think good thoughts.

"He's in town, and we don't want to judge him," she said. "We've always been welcoming to everyone. I think it would be a disservice to the town and also give Nolan an unfair view if you did anything different. Personally, I'm surprised you would take that view of Nolan. A lot of us came here as strangers, and we found a place. Nolan deserves the same opportunity that all of us had not to be judged on quick opinions but on his character and what he does."

Micah had stopped looking at her and was looking past her shoulder.

"Thank you, Layla." Nolan's voice came from behind her.

Had he been there for the whole speech? With her luck, yes, he had. It didn't make a difference. What she told Micah was true. Everyone deserved the benefit of the doubt.

"I couldn't say anything less about a person who is such a good neighbor," she said. "Besides, I always think it's important for people to make judgments on what's in front of them and not what happened in the past. Don't you agree?"

When he didn't answer right away, she turned around and once again found herself in his personal space, looking up at him. Once again, a nice breeze came by, and she was transported to last night when they were in his backyard. A little heat started in her stomach and spread throughout her whole body. She even started to get a little bit of a chill. Was she sick? Was there something else going on here? All over, the noise going on in the fair fell to the background, and the only thing that she could really see was Nolan.

She had to break out of this. He hadn't kissed her and hadn't touched her. He was just standing in her personal space. She had to remember who she was, what she was doing, and why Nolan was here.

"Nolan Taggert, this is Micah Hamilton. He owns the consignment shop."

Nolan nodded to the older man. "I've been in your shop. The one at the middle of the block with the large assortment of local crafts, is that right?"

Micah put on a large smile. "Yes, my store is in the center of Commerce Lane. Everyone who comes to Inheritance Bay stops by. Did you see anything in my shop that you liked?"

Layla wasn't sure if she should step in. She understood what Micah was doing; he wanted to test whether or not Nolan had actually been in the store. Just when she was sure she was going to have to jump in, Nolan spoke up.

"Yes, I was in the store, and I love the way you have the H-style layout. This is a very popular layout with successful stores. Did you come up with that on your own?"

"Yes, yes. I try to go to other places in other towns and see what works there and then use it in my store."

"A town needs someone to go out there and bring back new and fresh ideas. The town is very lucky to have you."

Nolan sounded sincere in his praise, and when Layla looked at him, she knew he was. It was just another thing about Nolan that didn't add up but made him so interesting. Micah continued to preen, and Nolan listened as if Micah were dispensing pearls of wisdom. How did this very rich man listen to Micah, who barely made what Nolan made in a day?

"Micah!" called out Mrs. Hamilton.

Everyone stopped to look at Micah's wife. She was small and petite with blonde hair, and her smile was in place and firm. She tapped her wrist and cleared her throat.

"I've got to be going, but it was good to talk to a fellow businessman."

Layla was more than just a little annoyed. Somehow,

Nolan had become best friends with Micah. Micah who thought she was somehow the problem in the town.

"Did you get to see all of the booths?"

"I've been walking."

"Well, I can take you so that you can see—"

"Layla, you know I don't expect you to stay with me the whole time. I know that you're here working, as well, right?"

Layla looked at him, and for a moment, she thought about telling him he was right and walking away. True, that Ryan had come by, and she didn't want to just abandon him. Besides, a lot of people came to see her and Ryan sitting there putting on the finishing touches of some piece of work that they would then sell.

The real issue here was that while there was truly work to do, none of it seemed to be as appealing as staying with Nolan. Again, the little warning bells went off in the back of her mind. She knew she should get up and leave him here. But this was something else. She knew she had to show him the best things about Inheritance Bay, and she couldn't do that from afar.

No, she would let Ryan take care of the stand today. The festival would run today and tomorrow, so she would just take over tomorrow's shift. Besides, if she said she was doing this for the town, then she could go ahead and not look too closely at any other reason she'd want to be traveling around with Nolan Taggert.

"It's no problem at all. I'll show you my favorite stops."

Ten

It was the perfect storm, and Nolan was standing in the middle of it. He was here to evaluate a town. But he found more reasons to be with Layla than anything else. He supposed he could have said this was a great day for him to be with her. The weather was holding up well, and there were so many people at the fair. This would have been exactly the kind of activity that he would like to see in any place that he was scouting.

The problem with the whole thing was that he wasn't really paying attention to the town. What really mattered to him was the woman who was pointing out booths excitedly, showing him all the things that she thought were so amazing.

She had already been around the world, and still, she took such joy in the funnel cake maker who made her own custom toppings. Every time he thought he knew Layla, she went ahead and showed him another version of herself. She challenged his preconceptions of town people.

She was emotionally and intellectually attractive.

Large brown eyes that seemed to pull him in and her hair—that she was constantly trying to keep into some kind of bun or tie, and still, strands defied any form of confines. She always had color in her cheeks as if she had just finished running from someplace or she was excited about something. Listening to her talk about things that she loved to do or what she saw left a freshness and innocence in it all.

What made it all the more exciting was that he knew she could sense there was something going on between them. Nolan hadn't been in a position when a woman denied an attraction between them. In fact, he had been in the exact opposite situation. Usually, when he ran into a woman, and she knew that there was some kind of attraction, she would try to capitalize on it.

Again there was the regret that came on the heels of such a great discovery. Meeting Layla now was the wrong time in the wrong place. What was even worse was there was a suspicion in the back of Nolan's head that once he told Layla that he had decided against putting Wealth Builders' center here, she would never want to see him again. He would be foolish not to wonder if her attraction had more to do with the possibility of a center being here in Inheritance Bay.

Layla ran ahead of him and brought him to another booth where a woman made handmade potholders. As she picked some up and showed them to him, all thoughts about if this was right or wrong left him. Right then, the only thing he really wanted to do was spend the day with this beautiful woman who seemed to be able to find the joy in everything.

They had walked through all of the exhibits when Layla suggested they take a walk on the beach. As they walked down the lane, several people called out to say hello to Layla. It was a testament to her ability to be nice to everyone. He was enjoying just basking in her glow when she stopped and looked ahead of them.

"Are we looking at your favorite sand spot?" he asked with a laugh.

"No, it seems as though we are about to meet somebody that you know, and I don't. I mean, if we go by the way they are smiling and making a beeline toward you is any indication."

Nolan gave her an odd look and then saw the couple in front of them. It was his father, Colin, and his mother. What were they doing here? Why was his dad with her? His mother, Ellen, was dressed in an all-white sundress. His dad was dressed in khaki pants and a white shirt. If he didn't know any better, they looked like they were there as a couple.

"Well, as it would happen, I do know both of those people," Nolan said.

Layla turned to him and waited for him to finish the sentence.

"The man is Colin, my foster dad. The woman standing with him is my birth mother."

Layla didn't even hesitate at the titles; instead, she took another look and then looked at him.

"Those sandals she has are to die for. I wonder if she'll tell me where she got them?"

Nolan was taken back by the question. He was so used to people asking questions about his foster dad or his mom, that when she asked about the shoes, he was lost. Normally, he would have turned them around and gone the other way, but that moment of indecision of not saying anything to Layla was all the opportunity she needed to go straight toward them. He didn't suppose he could turn around and go back to the house. That would be rude, and his father would definitely talk to him when he finally made it home. That was another thing, Colin hadn't been at his place, and no one had seen him at the diner. Maybe the accommodations at the Turtledove Inn were better than he thought that a man wouldn't come spend time with his son.

Nolan wasn't one to run away from a situation, so he followed Layla to meet his parents. Nolan couldn't have been but six strides behind Layla, but when he got there, they had already finished with the introductions. His mother stepped up to him and pulled him into a hug. He knew she could feel him stiffen in the embrace, but he didn't move away.

"It's so good to see you, Nolan, even if you didn't invite me."

Oh yes, one of his mother's more notable traits was that she had a way with words.

When he pulled back from his mother, his father stepped in and pulled him close, slapping him on the back in welcome. When he had finally freed himself from both of their embraces, he stood back and waited to see what would happen next. The first thing he noticed was the questioning gleam in his mother's eyes. He could imagine what him walking hand in hand with Layla looked like to her, and he hoped she didn't get any ideas stuck in her head or tell them to his dad.

"I see you came to see the Spring Festival?" his dad said. "Every town is doing something during this time of year, and I was impressed with this one."

"Well, thank you," Layla said. "I mean, I can't take credit for it all, but we try to do more each year."

Nolan looked at Layla and his dad and realized they had a lot in common. They were both easygoing, and life wasn't taken as a given. They enjoyed people, and people enjoyed them.

"It is so much better than what happens in Sunset Valley. It's all commercial with no real crafts. I feel like they ordered all of their crafts online," his mother said.

A runner came by and interrupted the focus of the conversation, but soon his mother looked at everyone and said, "You know we can take a seat and talk if you'd like to?"

Nolan wanted to stamp his foot. No, he didn't want to sit down and talk with his parents. In fact, he was trying to figure out if he could get away with saying he was sick and then leave the situation. He must have waited too long to answer, because Layla did.

"I'm so sorry. I would love to sit down, but I'm fostering some dogs at my house, and we need to get back before it's time for their walk."

"Of course, dear, that's fine. It's so good that you are volunteering and helping out with animals that are less fortunate."

"Well, we don't want to hold you up," Nolan's father said. "I'm sure you're going to go with Layla and be a good neighbor," his father said with a smile.

"Yes, you go ahead and be a good neighbor," his mother echoed.

Now it was time to leave. Both of his parents were looking at Layla as if she was something on the menu instead of just his next-door neighbor. What made the situation worse was that not too long ago, he had thought about Layla in a different light.

"It's time for us to go," he said, looping his arm through Layla's.

"I'll see you two around then," his mother said as he walked away.

"I think if you walk any faster, I'll have to jog, and then they will know for sure that we are running from them," she murmured.

"I'm sorry," Nolan said. "My parents were a surprise to see, and I wasn't ready to deal with them right now."

"Oh, I thought it was the way your mother was looking at us and planning her grandchildren," Layla said with a laugh.

"Ok, so it wasn't just me. Yes, we needed to get out of there as soon as possible."

Ellen watched her son practically run away from her. The woman was very nice, though. Brown hair, brown eyes, and she seemed very trim and fit. What was even more important was that it seemed as though Nolan didn't mind talking to Ellen. That was a big feat as far as Ellen was concerned. Whatever was going on between them, it was still in its early stages. She knew what young love looked like. The shame of it all was this would probably be the only time she got a chance to see it, and it was all by accident.

This was how past mistakes came to haunt a person. Ellen had to admit she was more than happy when Nolan had decided to let her back into his life. But she had to say that being in his life seemed like a superficial thing. Nolan would answer her calls, of course, and if she backed him into a corner, he would even go out with her in public. Everything seemed like it was a negotiated deal. When they were together, they spoke about the weather and acted like strangers.

Ellen would admit she was jealous. She was jealous of the relationship Nolan had with Colin. She drew a little line in the sand with her foot, hoping to be able to blink back the tears before they fell. She didn't know what she was expecting, but when Colin had called and said he wanted to go out, she felt like a young girl all over again. There was excitement in the pitter-patter of her heart. She had dressed in her casual-but-not-too-casual clothing. Ellen had only dabbed a little bit of makeup on her eyelids.

Colin had been calling a little more often in the last couple of months, and although it hadn't been said between them, it was as if they were starting all over again, two strangers finding common ground where there didn't seem to be any. Now that they had seen Nolan, she knew the day was going to take a different turn. Seeing Nolan brought back all of the secrets that were standing between them all.

What was she doing there? The time for her and Colin had passed. She needed to accept it.

"Ellen, are you ok?"

And that was Colin. He always put himself second. Colin was always the one to take the brunt of everything first.

"I think I'm ready to go home. Thank you for bringing me to the fair today. I just think it's best if I go home."

Ellen had looked up, thinking she was going to see a face full of understanding and compassion. Instead, she saw a man's face filled with disappointment and hurt.

"Whatever it is you want to do, Ellen, you know I'll give it to you."

"You would, wouldn't you?"

Colin turned and faced her. "I'm surprised you would even ask me that question. Not only would I, but I've done it for you in the past."

She didn't even stop to answer him. Ellen just walked right by Colin, going toward the steps to get off the beach. Every step she took, the past kept weighing down on her. She had that horrible sinking feeling in her stomach, and the nausea was rising in her throat. This was a mistake. It was all a mistake. She should have known better than to see Colin. The past was the past, and it couldn't be undone.

She could hear him behind her calling her name, but she kept walking. He had brought her out here to talk, and she had fallen apart at the first sight of Nolan. She felt Colin's hand on her forearm, and she stopped.

"Ellen? When do we stop running?"

Anger boiled up from her soul. Why was he doing this? "I'm not running, Colin. I'm going home. I'm going home so I can pull myself together. Is that alright?"

"It's always like this, Ellen. If we talk about it, we could get this out of the way."

"Get this out of the way," she repeated back to him. "Ok, Colin, if that's what you think is going to make this better, let's go ahead and talk about it."

"Good, Ellen I—"

"No, Colin, you don't get to talk. I get to talk first. Nolan is a successful man. More importantly, he's a good man. Do you know why he's a good man? It has nothing to do with me being his mother. You want to talk about the past and get all of the secrets out in the open? For what? What exactly would that give us?"

"It might give us some closure, Ellen. It might allow us to start to live our lives."

She didn't even try to wipe away the tears that she knew were rolling down her cheeks.

"Colin, I don't deserve to have a life. I gave up my son. I caved to what I thought everybody was going to think about me, and I gave up my son so the town I lived in wouldn't look down on me. I did what I thought was right for him, but in the dead of night, I know the truth. I had the choice of being ostracized by all who knew me and raising my son or giving up my son and being able to stay with my friends and family. I didn't choose my son Colin."

"You didn't choose your son, Ellen, but I chose him for us. We were both young. What did we know about what we were doing or what we weren't doing?"

"You knew enough to get our son."

"Will you ever tell Nolan?"

"Tell him what, Colin? Tell him how I chose wrong

but thank goodness his father came in on the white horse and saved him. He barely speaks to me now, Colin. What do you think would happen if I told him that? Your relationship with him might recover, but mine would be permanently broken."

"We could do this together," Colin said.

Ellen laughed. She wiped away the tears on her cheeks and looked up toward the sun, hoping that the late evening rays would be able to cleanse her soul.

"You know, when I found out, I was so confused. There were so many problems. How could I tell anyone that the person who was tutoring me, and was part of a seasonal worker family, was the father of my child? It wasn't an option for me to get rid of his baby. People had suggested it, but I loved you, and I loved the baby. In some of my braver moments, I thought about getting all of my money together and then running off to one of those shelters, but I didn't think I could do that, either. I did what I thought was best at the time. In hindsight, it turns out it was the best thing to do for Nolan. It just cost me my son."

"The past is the past, Ellen. We can choose how we live our future."

"Can we? I don't want to lose what I have with Nolan now, Colin."

"He's a good man. Sometimes he can be hard and pigheaded just like we were, but he's a good man. He'll understand the stupidity of youth, and he'll forgive us."

Ellen let out a deep breath and gave Colin a sad smile. "I know he's a good man. He's got the best of his father."

Colin pulled her into his embrace. She laid her head on

his shoulder and let the tears flow for all the times that she couldn't before. They had started seeing each other because Nolan was working too hard, and they were both concerned. Then they realized they were more than just concerned about Nolan; they still had feelings for each other. He rubbed her back and murmured nonsensical words into her ear. When she had finally composed herself, she pulled back and looked into Colin's eyes.

"You really think we should tell him?"

"Not only do I think we should tell him, I think we should do it together."

She saw the sincerity in his eyes, and it bolstered her. "Set up a time when we can have dinner, and then I'll tell him. That has got to be the condition. I have to tell him. I started this, and I want to end it."

He brushed back a strand of hair around her ear and then leaned down and kissed her on her forehead. "We'll do it together. Just like I plan for us to be going forward."

For the first time in a very long time, Ellen Taggert felt safe and not alone.

Eleven

Layla was right—day two was just as busy as day one. So many people showed up on day two that Layla thought maybe they had sent out the wrong dates to the other places. She ran out of standard items. She had to ask Ryan to bring some more things to the booth. All the while, she was thinking about Nolan.

What was it about that man that made him so hard to forget? She was frustrated with herself when she found herself looking over her shoulder to see if he was there. She gave everyone a smile, but when a lady stopped and wanted to tell her how she had purchased some of her pottery for her whole family, Layla knew it was going to be a long conversation.

She was about to settle down to the long conversation when she saw Chief Nicolas Terrell. He was stopping at each booth to do a check. When she saw the chief, she stretched her hand to get his attention.

"Excuse me, ladies, but I need to talk to the booth

owner," Chief Terrell said. The woman tittered next to the six-foot chief and then left.

"So this is what I'm regulated to, fishing you out of trouble with dangerous fans?" he said with a smile.

"No, it's not your only job, but I am very happy that you came to my rescue."

"The rumor is you have another kind of beau that should be rescuing you."

"Well, those rumors are grossly exaggerated," she said with a smile.

The real problem was that she wanted these rumors to be true.

"Ok, Layla, I won't tell the rest of the town that somehow you managed to find this rich guy and lose him in the small town of Inheritance Bay."

They both laughed.

"Well, if we're going to spread rumors, just let me say, I didn't lose him. He knew I had to work today."

"Does he know today is the food and dessert day?"

"No, I don't think I brought that up."

"Wow, it is true that men and women have way different priorities."

Around midday, Ryan had shown up to give her a break. Layla had gone over and gotten a funnel cake with the caramel topping that she really loved. It wasn't really food, but it was her favorite.

"So I'm wondering, are you willing to share with a neighbor?"

She knew who it was before she even turned. She wasn't going to look into the giddy feeling that she had right now. It had nothing to do with Nolan and everything to do with today being such a great sales day.

"Well, you would have to be some kind of neighbor for me to share my funnel cake."

"I planned ahead. I suspected you might not share, so I already ate."

"Did you make yourself something at home?"

Nolan smiled sheepishly. "No, I didn't. I actually ate something at the other end of the lane."

"Good tactic, good tactic," Layla said.

"However, now that I am looking at your cake, I have to say, it looks tasty."

"The line is short. Go get one. By the time you come back, I'll be ready to share with you, neighbor," she teased.

Nolan smiled. "Fine, I'll be the good neighbor and bring you the backup funnel cake because I'm just that kind of guy," he joked.

"We all know just what kind of guy you are, Mr. Taggert."

Layla looked behind Nolan and someone she had never seen before in her life. The man was about the same size as Nolan, and he had a sign in his hand that said Stop the Reaper. It seemed as though the universe was going to send her a sign to remind her just who Nolan was. What his job was and that no matter how good the man seemed, he had a job, and that job threatened those she loved in the town.

It was one thing for someone to come looking for Nolan, but if a fight started in the middle of the festival, it would ruin it for everyone. She put her funnel cake down and stood up to stand in front of Nolan and hopefully deflect the situation before it got so loud that everybody was looking. This protester had already been asked to leave peaceably and refused; Layla thought it was only a matter of time before he took it to the next level.

"I'll come looking for you, Mr. Reaper. You probably don't even know who I am."

"I know who you are, Cresswell," Nolan replied.

Layla could see the man was shocked that Nolan even knew his name. During that moment of his speechlessness, she tried to get in between the men to try to defuse the situation.

"Mr. Cresswell, please, I'm not really sure what the issue is, but this is a friendly outing, and this is not the place for it."

"Move aside, little woman. You don't know what the Reaper is or what he does. He goes to small towns and then guts them of their small town air and makes them into human factories, or he finds good people that can't hold on to places that have been in their family for generations, buys them for centers or the such," Cresswell spat. "The Reaper doesn't care. He just takes and takes until there's nothing left. My town used to be a place where people came, and there were dreams. When the Reaper was done, it was a ghost town. He wreaked havoc in a day."

"It wasn't a day. The transition took seven months. We offered everyone fair value for the houses and for their land," Nolan said. "We dealt fairly with everyone who was there. There were some situations where people couldn't move, and still, we let them stay there even though the city had already sold their tract of land."

Layla listened to Nolan defend himself. She had to remember this was what he normally did. But once again, Nolan had added a new dimension to her vision, so he wasn't the cold-hearted and calculating person she thought he was.

Cresswell looked at Layla with wild eyes. "You can't believe him. I was happy in my town. My wife was with me when we had the house. Everything was going well, and then he came. We didn't want to move. We didn't want to do anything brand new. When Wealth Builders came, though, they took what they wanted. It wasn't about money. It should have been about people."

Layla felt bad for Cresswell. He had obviously lost so much, but she could tell that Nolan had offered compensation and something fair. Layla knew that right now, Cresswell would not be able to hear a thing. He was blinded by grief. She was also scared to say anything to push him over the edge. Nolan seemed to have it all under control.

"I didn't pick your town because it was easy-picking. Wealth Builders makes it a habit only to choose towns that are economically disadvantaged with no other options. Your town had already borrowed three times from the county in order to make its basic payments. When we see small-town America struggling, sometimes Wealth Builders can help by putting a center in that town. I mean, sometimes there is no help for it, and we just buy up the land. You may not want to hear this right now, but if we had not come, something else would have happened because there was no money, and the town couldn't keep going living on debt."

Each word seeped into Cresswell's demeanor. Every fact that Nolan brought up made Cresswell's back get stiffer. Anger and shame seemed to wash over him.

"You don't know a thing! My wife left after you took our land and our farm. We were never the same, and she left—" Cresswell said with tears running down his cheeks.

Layla sensed that this had gone on long enough. She had to step in and do something before this snowballed into an event that ruined everything.

"You know what, Nolan?" Cresswell continued. "The worst of it is that you're not even sorry. You go around the country in your big plane and your expensive suit, and you ruin peoples' lives. You just leave them like roadkill, and you keep on going."

Then it all happened so quickly. Cresswell took a step forward. Layla turned, so she was facing him. She thought she heard Cresswell say something like he wasn't going to take this anymore. She lifted up her arms to get his attention, but the only thing that did was aggravate him. The next thing she knew, Cresswell had grabbed her by the shoulder and pushed her to the side. She hadn't realized how strong the man was until after she felt herself falling to the side.

She heard a firm and low voice say, "Enough." She hadn't seen Nolan, and the voice had such a ferocity to it that she thought it could only be Nolan who would make that kind of stand in the town. The other option was that someone else had come with Cresswell and that didn't bear thinking about. Then the ground rushed up to meet her.

Moments later, she was trying to push herself up, and

then the next thing she knew, she saw Cresswell on the ground with her, as well. She didn't know how he had gotten there, but she was willing to bet it wasn't of his own accord.

Then she felt two strong arms lifting her up off the ground and pulling her into a warm embrace. This was exactly the wrong time to be feeling like the saved girl from a movie. That being said, Layla felt amazing right then. Somehow she was being saved. When was the last time a man had saved her? True, her timing was off as usual, but she had to admit being held in Nolan's arms was amazing. Then she thought about the whole town watching her being held in his arms, cradled against his chest, safe from the grieving Cresswell.

And that was when it happened. In one moment, Nolan had gone from being an outsider to being a member of Inheritance Bay. She heard him calling out to people to come and move Cresswell, and everyone obeyed him. He didn't make a scene, and he kept his voice low. When Layla looked up from inside his arms, she saw people going around doing his bidding, and the fair didn't seem to notice one way or the other.

There was one more time. Just when she thought she knew Nolan, he went and did something that was totally nice and heroic and made him all the more lovable.

Nolan once again found himself off-kilter when dealing with Layla. The whole Cresswell event had come out of nowhere, but at the end of it, he had Layla in his arms. There was something about having Layla in his arms, but he was trying not to look too closely at it. Layla just felt right there. When she looked up at him, her eyes were soft, her body was pliant, and the world seemed to fall away. In the next moment, the warm woman who had been in his arms transformed into the prickly neighbor he had met on day one.

He knew Layla wasn't the type of woman to try to lead him on, and so he was at a total loss. What was going on? What was he missing? What did this even matter? Nolan knew that this attraction couldn't go anywhere. He had too much respect for Layla to make her think he was going to do anything but leave when this assignment was done. He knew she wanted his cake, but he wanted to eat it, too. He wanted to spend some time with an amazing woman, but he didn't want her to think that it would ever be anything more than just today.

How could he have met Layla now? She was the kind of woman you expected to be married right away. She had left him and went with Chief Terrell to take Cresswell to the jail. The evening had come, and they were supposed to meet to watch the wrap-up fireworks for the Spring Festival.

As far as Nolan was concerned, all the fireworks had already happened earlier today. Maybe this meeting really wasn't such a good idea, and he should find a way to cancel. Nolan kept the thought firmly in his mind until he saw Layla coming toward him. She was dressed in an orange sundress that flowed about her ankles. There was something fresh and new about her, and he knew tonight they would explore what might be between them, and he wasn't going to walk away from the opportunity of being with her under the stars.

"Maybe we should have gone to the beach tonight, Layla. I hear a lot of people have gone there to watch the fireworks."

"They have, and that's the number one reason why we're not going. You'll always find someone on the beach who decides that they can have a better firework display than the one that's being put on."

"I guess that falls under small town improvisation?"

Layla shook her head. "No, it just falls under teens thinking they can do anything. I remember being that age and thinking it would be so great if we lined up four or five rocket launchers together and lit them with one fuse."

"Wow, that is scary."

Layla shrugged her shoulders. "That's what happens when you're young, and you believe you're invincible."

"Did the rest of the town let you get away with that?"

"So we're going to go back to interrogating me about how I came here?"

Nolan shrugged. "I hope you don't think this is an interrogation. I'm just curious to know everything about you. You seem to understand how small towns work."

"Well, I don't mind telling you, but we're going to have to get off the main path. I think I see some benches. We can sit on those and watch the fireworks at the same time."

They walked over to the benches, and Nolan watched as everyone gave them a wide berth. It wasn't just that Layla had changed after the incident earlier today, but the townspeople had changed their attitude toward him, as well. It was something that he was still trying to reconcile, and he definitely wasn't feeling very comfortable about it.

Walking through Inheritance Bay and not having suspicious looks tossed at him but instead a small nod here, or there was a new experience for him. He had to admit there was something comforting about having nonverbal communication and knowing all of these people, for whatever reason, were supporting him and knew him.

They had both taken a seat on the bench when Nolan turned to Layla and waited.

"So the rest of my story. The short version is my brother and me, and my mom came and were accepted by Inheritance Bay, and we lived happily ever after."

Nolan laughed. "Those were all of the juicy details?"

"Well, I figure that until you can explain to me the tension that was on the beach the other day when we ran into your parents, I've given you way more information. At this point, Nolan Taggert, you owe me."

"You might be right. If it's any consolation, I'm working up to it."

Just then, they heard two or three fireworks go off in the distance. They both jumped to their feet, but they didn't see any lights in the sky.

"Do you think there's a problem?" Nolan asked.

Layla shook her head.

"No, it's always like this. They do a test right before, so the fireworks should be starting in about fifteen minutes." Layla turned so that she was facing him and then tapped him on the shoulder. "I wanted to talk about this afternoon."

Nolan looked at Layla, and all at once, he felt horrible.

"Here you are out with me, and I didn't even ask if you are ok. I saw you take the tumble to the ground, and I should have made sure that you were ok to come out tonight."

Layla smiled and then looked away. "What am I going to do with you, Nolan Taggert?"

"Well, the first thing you need to remember is to never jump in between me and some other guy who's distressed. I can handle that kind of situation."

"Do you think I would let someone just come out of nowhere and accuse you of things, Nolan? It's true, I know we haven't known each other for a long time, but the things he was saying were too far off for you to have actually done."

Nolan looked down to soft brown eyes, and he tried to remember the last time a woman had stuck up for him. It was endearing and sweet and unnecessary, but still, there was something about it.

"Don't paint me as an angel, Layla. I want you to know I've done my fair share of things that might make you look at me twice."

"I think that at your core, you're a good guy."

Nolan would never be able to say what happened after that moment or where his thoughts went. He just knew looking down into her brown eyes with her smiling at him, having faith and confidence in him, she proved to be an irresistible treat that he was tired of fighting. Nolan Taggert did the unthinkable. He pulled Layla into his arms, and in the middle of the fair, he kissed her.

Twelve

His arms felt great the second time around. That first time being wrapped up against his chest was not a one-off. Nolan Taggert had the goods to be a knight in shining armor. Here she was kissing the man as if they were the only ones out there. Nolan had the power to reduce her back to the caution of a teenager. For goodness' sake, she fell on her shoulder, not her head. There was no excuse for her languishing in Nolan's arms.

Besides the regular heat flooding through her body and the taste of funnel cake still on his lips. This moment was perfectly…wrong. She had to think of the town, and she was going to in just a minute. Layla was going to indulge in the kiss for just a moment more. Like everything else about Nolan, she felt like she had been swept up into a whirlwind and could do anything as long as they were together.

Together?

The word acted like a bucket of ice water tossed at her. There was no together. He was here to do a job, and she was supposed to be looking out for her family, not indulging in some silly school girl moments. When she pulled away from him, she still had to hold on to his shoulders. One couldn't just jump off of a roller coaster, at least not safely. Layla had already caused enough attention to be tossed her way.

"I think that this is a sign that I've got to go."

"Because?"

What could she possibly tell him? But her will was weak around him. That when she kissed him, she wondered if she was being unfaithful to the town.

"I think that if you stay here, Nolan, you'll still have a great view of the fireworks."

Nolan laughed. "I think I've already gotten the show, thank you."

Layla looked at him and shook her head. "Is there a book of cheesy lines that all guys use?"

"There isn't a book. We just all have a cheesy gene built-in."

They both laughed, and then she took a step out of his arms. "I didn't before, but I wanted to say thank you. Thank you for taking care of things after Cresswell pushed me."

"Maybe I should be telling you thank you, Layla. It was a new experience for me, and I have to tell you, there was something enjoyable about telling the people in the town what to do."

"You do that all the time at your company. What was different?"

"I don't have to pay any of the people in Inheritance Bay, and they did it anyway for the greater good of the town."

"Be careful, Nolan. It's starting to sound like you like small towns."

Nolan shrugged. "Maybe I'm just wrapped up in the local talent."

"Well, on that note, I'm going to be making a tactical retreat."

"I thought you didn't run, Layla?" Nolan said with a smile.

"This isn't a retreat. This is regrouping. Prepare yourself, Nolan, and I haven't forgotten you will be giving me the details on this whole parent situation. I've got to go. Stay, watch the fireworks, the ones in the sky."

Layla didn't wait for him to respond. She wasn't sure she could keep up the banter anymore. No, she was in way too deep, and right now, what she needed to do was to have someone who had more sense than she did to see this situation clearly. It was obvious. She needed a doctor.

Layla knew that Carrie was here tonight. She just needed to find her. It had taken everything Layla had in her not to run away from Nolan. As she looked through the fair, she found everyone except Carrie. She knew Carrie had set up a medical center just in case there were any problems during the fair. Just when she thought she wouldn't be able to find her, finally, she saw the red-and-white tent. She rushed into the tent to find that Carrie was alone.

"Hey, what are you doing here? Is your shoulder bothering you?" Carrie asked.

"No, my shoulder is fine. That's not it."

"I'm sorry I missed all the excitement. You know there was someone who had gotten sick, then there was someone else who stuck themselves with one of the skewers. It has just been a popping day all day long and then—"

"Carrie, I need you to listen to me. I have a problem."

Carrie walked behind her and then closed the door to the tent, zipping it down. After that, she went to sit on one of the cots and patted the space right next to her.

"So, go ahead and tell me about your six-foot-one, rich problem."

"How did you know?"

"There were some big hints. You came rushing into the tent, and there's nothing wrong with you. Your hair is out of place—more so than normal—and your lips are a little puffier. Since you didn't come in here to tell me that you have finally discovered an allergy to some fruit, I can only assume that you and our visitor are getting a lot closer than you thought."

Layla just dropped her head into her hands and tried to think about how she had gotten into this mess. It was Nolan Taggert, for goodness' sake. There was no future there—there was nothing there—and still, she found herself falling for this man more and more every day.

What the last couple of days had shown her was that all the things she wanted to believe about him were wrong. He wasn't callous. He did care about people. She sat up and ran her hands through her hair. Closing her eyes, she took a deep breath and let it out. What did it even matter? He wasn't going to stay. Nolan Taggert didn't like small towns.

"So I can tell from your silence this is more than just a kiss. Tell me you had the foresight to have this kiss in a closet away from peering eyes?"

Layla moaned. "I didn't have enough wherewithal to consider where we were. Besides, I wasn't the one who started to kiss."

"Oh, and now all of the juicy details start to come out. She says she wasn't the one who started the kiss, but that does imply she was the one who continued the kiss."

Layla looked up to see a wide smile on Carrie's face. "You're supposed to be helping me?"

Carrie reached out and grabbed Layla's hand. She placed her other hand atop of that and patted.

"I am here to help you, Layla. I want to make sure that you're happy. I think you need to really consider why Nolan makes you happy. You weren't born here, so it's not the same for you. You have options. You could leave and go live in the city, or you could stay here with us. It's one of the things that I've always admired, and I have to admit I've also been a little jealous of. I was born and raised here in Inheritance Bay. I could never think about leaving. You, on the other hand, have options. And if Nolan Taggert makes you happy, I hope you keep yourself open to those options."

"What am I going to do, Carrie? He's not exactly here to find a new home."

Carrie nodded her head. "I know. So maybe what you need to do is to forget why he's here and just talk to the man."

"The man?"

Carrie stood up and nodded at Layla. "Yeah, you know,

the man it seems you've fallen in love with."

"Don't say it out loud."

Carrie laughed. "Is that supposed to keep the truth at bay?"

"Ugh! I don't know, but I'm willing to try anything right now."

"Listen, why don't you come out with us for dinner?"

"No, I've gotta go take care of Princess."

"You can take care of her, and then come over. We'll save you a spot."

"Maybe?"

Layla knew she wouldn't be joining Carrie and the crew for dinner. She heard Carrie unzip the tent and then call over her shoulder.

"Remember, Layla, you need to make sure you do what's right for you. That's all anyone in this town would ever want for you."

Layla let Princess out into the backyard. Princess gingerly stepped out of the basket and onto the ground. She didn't go far, but she had climbed out of the basket to touch the cement in the backyard. It was a step. Layla wondered if that was all it took, just a step in the right direction.

"You didn't stay for the fireworks?"

The sound of his voice made her standstill. Her heartbeat started to accelerate, and all of a sudden, the world focused just on the deep timbre of his voice. She looked behind her, and there he was, Nolan Taggert.

"Princess needed to go out."

"Do you normally stay at the booth when they wrap up?"

"Ryan and I like to take the wrap-up fireworks as an opportunity to flip down our booth so that we don't have to be caught in the crush."

"And tonight?"

"Tonight, Ryan is going to take care of the booth, and I decided that maybe I needed a little me time."

"I'm sorry, am I interrupting?"

Well, that was the million-dollar question. Carrie's words floated through Layla's mind. Maybe it was time for her to do something for herself. It was true there were no guarantees in life, and meeting Nolan was definitely not on the radar. She took a deep breath and was greeted by a warm breeze that flowed over her. The air was filled with the smell of popcorn and funnel cakes, and you could hear the light echoes of people laughing and fireworks in the background. Maybe it was time for more than just Princess to take a chance and step out on her own.

"Were you planning to go in for the night, Nolan?"

"No."

"Well, then come on over. I'll start the grill up, and this time, I'll throw some steaks on the grill for you."

"You don't have to. I know you said you were coming to get some you time. I completely understand how important that is."

Again, Nolan had shocked her with his compassion.

"It's ok, you can come over. How else am I going to grill you about your life and your mother if you're not here, and I'm not filling you with food?"

"Ugh! Are we back to that subject again? I don't know. Do you have really good steaks over there? Of all the topics I want to talk about with a beautiful woman, my parents or my mother are definitely not in the top twenty."

Had he just called her beautiful?

"Stop stalling. I'm going to go put Princess up. I'll open the back gate, and you can come on in."

She had put Princess up in record time. Layla once again gave herself a look over. She thought about changing into a dress, but that would seem too obvious. So here she was in a white t-shirt and cut-off blue jeans going to sit with a man for dinner. She stopped by the refrigerator, and pulled out the steaks that she had at the bottom. Normally, after the festival, Ryan would come over. However, every since Nolan had come, Ryan and her hadn't been seeing as much of each other as she would have liked. She knew her baby brother was sulking. It didn't matter. When Nolan was gone, he would get over it—that is, if Nolan left.

The steaks were on the tray, and she went back up to the yard only to find Nolan sitting comfortably in a chair waiting for her. Without saying a word, she went ahead and turned on her grill, put the steaks on the side plate, and then went back in the house to get a pot of rice. She was so grateful that she had let Ryan buy what he called a real man grill. It had two decks in order to cook steaks, and it had three eyes on the side to put pots so she could cook rice or pasta if she wanted to. Tonight was just going to be rice and steak. She had some salad in the refrigerator, and she'd bring that out last. When she was sure she had everything under control and started, she went and took a seat next to Nolan at the round, white patio table.

"Alright, buddy, I'm ready. It's time for you to give me the exclusive tell-all."

"Are you really interested in that? I think talking about that is going to be a huge downer. I mean, we could talk about other uplifting historical things like World War One or World War Two."

"You know, Nolan, I wasn't sure how you were going to try to do it, but I knew you were going to try to get out of this exchange of information. What was it that I said to you before? You are a closed book. Besides, you know everything there is to know about me and how I got here. Why I like the town of Inheritance Bay, and even why I came back."

Nolan groaned and held his hands out in defense.

"Fine, fine, fine. You win. Where did all of that tenacity come from, Layla?"

Layla smiled. "I'm one-hundred percent sure it came from my mom."

Nolan folded his hands on the patio table and then looked at them for a moment. The silence stretched on, and the only thing that could be heard was the slight sizzle coming from the grill. She had been so intent on finding out about this man she had been falling for, but now she felt she had been insensitive to him.

"I know I can seem like a dog with a bone, but please, if it's going to be this hard for you, maybe we shouldn't talk about it."

Nolan looked up at her and gave her a small smile. "You know, the funny thing is that this really shouldn't bother me. It's all in the past, and it doesn't have any power over me but—"

Layla nodded her head. "Sometimes we think we've gotten over things in the past. It may just come up at the oddest times. So if you don't want to talk about this, I totally get it."

"Nope, I don't run, not even from myself. So let's see. Let's start at the beginning. I already told you I was given up for adoption."

"Your dad adopted you? He seems so young."

Nolan nodded. "Well, it didn't exactly happen that way. When I was first growing up, I actually was with Colin's mother, who I have always called my grandmother. Abuela Maria was my mother. What I should say is she's the one who really raised me from birth until I was five. As she got sick, Colin was always around, and then when she finally passed away, I guess they took care of the paperwork, and Colin fostered me and then adopted me."

"Wow, you were really fortunate."

"It's true, I was. I can tell you that I often read stories about other kids who were in foster care or adopted, and I could never relate. I was always in a loving home. At any rate, Colin adopted me, and he was my father. I've never looked at him as anything less."

Layla reached out and placed her hands on top of Nolan's.

"He seems like a really good man. Your life has been charmed to a certain degree, Nolan. Although it seems like bad things might have been happening, good situations came out of them."

"You're right. It was all actually going very well until I hit my teens. Then my mother showed back up. At first, I didn't want to have anything to do with her. I figured she had already made her decision and chosen her life. But my father told me I should give her a chance because I wasn't in her position."

Layla heard Nolan say the words, but his voice was tense, and his hands were clasped tightly together. She couldn't begin to imagine what it must have cost his father to tell him to go see his mother and what it cost Nolan just to obey the man he had always known as his father. She wanted to move closer to him and pull him into her arms; instead, she sat still and listened.

"So I must have been fifteen when I went to see her for the first time in Sunset Valley. The problem wasn't seeing her. The problem was that she had already been married, and there were two other children in the house."

"You have stepbrothers and sisters?"

"The children belong to her husband. She never had any children after me."

"Oh."

Layla's heart ached for Nolan's mother. It couldn't have been easy for her to live in a house with two other children knowing that her child was somewhere out there and wasn't with her.

"So when I found out there were other children living with my mother, I do what all teens do. I decided to rebel. I didn't want to see her. My dad wanted me to go ahead and keep in contact with her. I had decided that if she liked those kids better than me, then what was the point? Those were some rough years."

"Did you ever talk to your mother and ask her what had happened?"

"No. I never asked why she wanted the other kids and didn't want me. In the beginning, it was because I was scared she was going to actually have an answer and tell me that there was something wrong with me. As time went on, I decided it didn't matter. The only one who really mattered was my dad."

"I'm so sorry, Nolan. But it seems that all of you were victims in this. There are never good options when it comes to broken families. We all get there for different reasons and different paths, but it always seems like everyone is hurt in the aftermath."

"I know that my mother was a victim in all of this. She was a young woman in a time that was more restrictive about teenage pregnancy, and rationally, I totally understand what happened. But there was something about the little boy me that didn't. To that little boy, she had made a decision, and I had lost."

"You're grown now, Nolan. Doesn't it mean now we talk things out and find out what happened?"

"So let me finish telling this story."

"Oops, sorry. Go on. Let me go flip the steaks, or we're going to be peeling charcoal off of good meat."

Layla ran to the grill, turned off the rice, and then flipped the steaks and put the grill on low. She went back to the patio and got comfortable in her seat.

"Ok, I'm ready."

"So when I started to really move up at Wealth Builders and built myself a career, my father decided he didn't want anyone to know that he was my father."

"What? I don't understand."

"You weren't the only one. So from twenty to twenty-six, I now had a bigger chip on my shoulder, thinking neither one of my parents wanted me."

"Ouch!"

"Finally, my dad told me he didn't want people to hold anything against me because his family was a bunch of seasonal workers who moved from state to state. I told him that I didn't care, but he was adamant about it until I had gotten to a certain point in my career. It's only until very recently that I've actually been able to bring my dad out and introduce him as my father. I always thought my mother spoke to my father and made that a condition."

"Nolan, that's horrible. What would make you think such a thing?"

"When I was younger, I overheard a couple of conversations. It was always so odd to me, but my dad would call my mother. I just always thought it was because he was a good man. All of the conversations I ever heard between them were about him agreeing to get me to talk to her and about how they would have to own up together. When I wasn't interested in doing that, and he was pushing me toward her had made no sense at the time, but now in retrospect, it seemed to all click together."

"Did you talk to your father?"

Nolan laughed mirthlessly. "It's not a thing to talk to my dad about my mom. He gets to a certain point, and then he just says, 'You know what, I just think you need to spend some time with your mother.' So I did what all kids do. I spent the least amount of time with her, and I threw myself into my career."

"But what I hear is a lot of misunderstanding and unsaid things going on between the three of you. I'm not one to tell you what to do, but I miss my mom every day. When you don't have your parents anymore, all the things that you were fighting about seem so insignificant. Whatever happened in the past happened, but your parents are both here today. If they can get past it in order to be with one another, then maybe you need to get past it in order to hear them out."

Nolan was still focused on his hands. She could see the white of his knuckles and knew she had pushed him as far as she was going to today. She got up and went to the grill so she could serve out the steaks and the rice.

"So, tell me, Dr. Layla, I feel like this is a natural part of your personality."

"Which part?" Layla asked as she turned off the grill and turned to get the plates.

"The I want to reach out and help everybody syndrome."

When Layla turned, he was standing right behind her. This time there was no denying what was about to happen. Nolan threaded his hands through her hair and tilted her head to the side. His head came down, and when he was a breath away, he said, "Layla?"

She could have told him no or just pushed him away if he had just kissed her, but even now, when he was in control and had the upper hand, he was considerate.

"Yes," Layla whispered. The first kiss was a banging at the door. This kiss was a slow discovery and languid journey of tenderness. His lips gently went over hers, and his care baked a slow flame within her. Her arms came up around his shoulders, and when her hands were anchored there, he pulled her deeper into his arms.

This was what it felt like to be held by a man you loved. Once upon a time, she had thought she was in love. She remembered what those kisses felt like, and by comparison, they paled to this moment. This kiss made it clear she was past the point of trying to figure out if she cared. It was just a matter of finding out how she was going to protect herself when he left.

Nolan broke the kiss, and then she leaned against his chest as she caught her breath.

"Well, let me be the first one to say that you have definitely been investing your time in more than just your career. It seems you have put significant effort in perfecting kissing, as well."

"I don't know if I put a lot of time into it; maybe it's just the partner I'm with."

Layla looked at him and then shook her head.

"Your partner doesn't have as much experience as you might think."

"Then maybe it's true, sometimes you have to stick people together who would never be together in order to get great results. Personally, I'm not feeling as confident as you are about this whole kissing thing. I'm always traveling and working. I'm thinking I could definitely do with a refresher course."

"I think this is as far into the pool as I get to wade. I'm going to make us some food, and we're going to sit down as if we were just neighbors."

"Is that what you want?"

Why was he asking these questions? *Is that what I*

want? What Layla wanted right now and what made the most sense were definitely at odds with one another.

"I don't see a relationship in our future, Nolan."

"So you have to be able to see everything, is that right, Layla?"

"Yes," she whispered.

"Does it all need to be planned out for you? Can you just play this by ear?"

For a moment, Layla actually let that thought run through her mind. Could she just play this by ear? Could she just enjoy Nolan for whatever time she would have him?

"I think that would be a horrible idea, Nolan."

"Wow, not even bad, it's horrible. You want to tell me how I got into the horrible category?"

"Turns out that's a really simple question to answer. I know I really like you, Nolan. I also know that you're not here on vacation or to recharge. You're here to make a final judgment on all the people who have made up my life for the last thirty-plus years."

"We're not talking about Inheritance Bay; we're talking about us. We're talking about two adults who've just discovered they like each other."

Layla smiled. "I'm sure you see it that way. But the problem here is that the man who likes me would also like my family, and Inheritance Bay is my family. I have to tell you, life was a lot simpler when I thought you were the evil man next door who had come to strip the town. Now I know that you are a sweet and compassionate and responsible man, nothing like the creature I thought you were when I first met you."

"At least I'm getting some pluses on the humanity scale. I can't tell you I'm not a sore loser, but I'm always going to respect all of your decisions. Why don't we do this: We've got some steaks but do them some justice. Then you can tell me how your day was today at the booth."

And there it was again. She had expected him to be upset or to try to convince her that maybe there was a way, but not Nolan. Instead, he graciously accepted and respected her decision. Instead of stomping away like a petulant child, he stayed the evening. He ate the salad, the steak, and the rice. They spoke to each other like they were friends. When he had finally left and gone back home, Layla could feel the loss.

Nolan Taggert was a man any woman could love.

Thirteen

Last night had not gone the way Nolan thought it would. Still, he woke up the next morning feeling refreshed. He had to admit that bringing his laptop out to the backyard and doing some of the work here under the cool breeze and the fresh air was the change in scenery he needed.

He didn't think he was going to go so far as to tell Connor that he was right about having to take this vacation. In fact, he suspected that the reason his father hadn't come to the rental with him and was staying at Turtledove had all been part of a larger plot so that he would be sure he stayed and tried to relax.

He had just brought his laptop into the house when he heard someone knock on the back gate in the yard. It was around lunchtime, and he was hoping that it was Layla. They were making it a habit to cook for one another, and he had to admit he was looking forward to seeing her. When he stepped out into the backyard, though, all of his hopes went by the wayside. It wasn't Layla. It was his mother.

Layla's words came back and haunted him as he saw his mother step into the backyard. She should have known that, of course, she could step into her son's backyard. There should have been a confidence and surety that he knew his father had when he came to visit. Still, she gingerly stepped in and waited by the closed gate.

"Mom," he said as he stepped out into the backyard.

"Hi, Nolan. I was at the front of the house, and I rang the doorbell and knocked, but no one came. I was just taking a chance to see if you were in the backyard."

"You must have just missed me. I've been working, and I just took all of my equipment back into the house."

His mother looked around, and then he realized his manners were lacking.

"Please, come in and take a seat."

It was as if she let out a sigh. Had their relationship gotten to the point that his mother wasn't sure if she was welcome around him?

"I was a little nervous coming here, Nolan. I mean, I wasn't sure if you would be entertaining."

"Oh, you mean Layla?"

"Yes, Layla."

"We're just neighbors, and she has been really helpful to me since I got here by showing me around and such."

"Oh, well, that's good."

Then both of them were startled when they heard Layla calling from her backyard.

"Nolan, I've got some more steaks, and I don't think I'm going to be—" Layla stopped mid-sentence when she saw his mother sitting in the backyard. "I'm so sorry, I didn't realize anybody was with Nolan. It's no problem.

I was just going to bring over some steaks, but I can do it later."

Ellen Taggert stood up. "Please, don't let me stop you."

"No, no, it's no worries. Nolan is always here anyway. Normally, he's out here slaving away under the beautiful weather. I'll come back later."

Layla excused herself quickly, and then his mother turned and looked at him with a raised eyebrow.

"So she's just a neighbor, huh?"

Nolan was still too raw from last night, and he couldn't really discuss Layla. Least of all, could he discuss Layla with his mother?

"How can I help you, ma'am?"

"Is that all there is, Nolan? How can you help me, or what can you give me, and then I can move along out of your life?"

"No," he processed it quickly.

Ellen shook her head and then turned to leave.

"This was a bad idea from the go, and I'm so sorry that I barged in on you."

"Mom, please. Why don't you have a seat? I'll bring us something to drink."

She turned around and gave him a long look, and then took a seat on the patio furniture. When he came back out with the tray, he found his mother sitting at the patio table but wringing her hands together in her lap. He wondered what had her in such a nervous frenzy.

"Mom, is everything alright?"

"Well, it really isn't, but life is more complicated the longer you live."

"Ok, I'm not quite sure what all that meant, but whatever it is, you can tell me."

Ellen stopped wringing her hands and looked up at Nolan. "Can I really tell you anything, Nolan? You know, I sometimes wonder that if I say the wrong thing to you, you'll leave. You get your final payback against me and do the same thing I did to you when you were a child. You just decide that I shouldn't be in your life."

Nolan shook his head. "You're human, Mom. And at the end of the day, no matter what happens, you're still my mother. I don't have to like everything that you do, but I don't want you to worry that I'm ever going to turn my back on you."

Ellen wiped away a tear that was going down her cheek.

"Well, I think I'm about to test that."

Now Nolan was feeling tense and on edge. He wasn't sure what it was, but he just wanted Ellen to spit it out.

"First, I want to tell you that your father and I are seeing each other."

Nolan laughed and then sat down, allowing the tension to leave his body.

"I know that, Mom. I think it's a little odd, but I know that."

"Well, the thing about it that isn't odd is that we are just picking up from where we originally left off."

"I don't understand."

"What I'm trying to tell you, Nolan, is that Colin is not your adopted father or your foster father. He is your biological father."

Nolan stopped, and everything he thought he knew

shattered around him. All of a sudden, all of the time that Nolan had caught his father on the phone talking to his mother came back to him. All of the conversations started to piece together, and now it all made sense. Even the part where he had told Layla about being placed with his Abuela all made sense.

"The both of you have known all of this time. Obviously, you both knew, so why tell me now?"

"I know this is going to sound horrible, but I asked your father the same thing. He insisted if we were going to have a relationship and be able to move forward, that we shouldn't have secrets between family. I was the one who made him not tell you. We had so many problems. I thought I would lose you."

"Dad let you come and tell me this by yourself?"

"No, he thought we should do it together. I thought since I was the one who made all of these decisions, that I needed to get my big girl bloomers on and come and tell you the truth. We're not in this position because of anything your father did. We're in this place because your father respected all of my wishes, no matter how ill-advised they were."

Nolan's voice was calm, but inside, there were a million thoughts swirling around. A million memories were coalescing into things that now made sense.

"So this has come about because you two are dating, and you want to go back to what we might have had if we had been a family?"

"No. I am not so naïve to think that things are just presto fixed like that, Nolan. I just wanted you to be prepared to see us together, or if that's too much for you, we can make sure we don't visit you when we are together. Your father would like to have dinner with you and me so we can go over it and see how we all feel."

Then another thought came to him. He had to ask it, and if it were true, it would be the nail in the coffin on the number of things he could endure for now.

"Did you know that dad was at the Turtledove Inn? Were you with him?"

He saw his mother look away and then straighten her back and look him in the eye. "Your father was at the inn two days ago. Since then, he has been with me." With that statement, Ellen Taggert stood up. Nolan stood up from habit and manners.

"If you're okay with dinner, let your father know. I think I need to give you some processing time, so I'll leave."

Processing time? Nolan wasn't sure that he could process anything right now. Just the whole idea of thinking about what all of this meant was hurting his brain. Before long, he had walked his mother out to the front, and she had gotten into her car. It wasn't until he felt her hand on his that he jumped out of his own reverie to focus on her face.

"I love you, Nolan. It's true. I mean, I haven't been the best mother or even made the best decisions, but I've always tried to tell you the truth no matter what. The truth is I love you, Nolan, and I don't want to lose you. Think about dinner and let your father know."

He stood in front of the house as he watched his mother drive away. What had just happened here? All the things that he thought he knew were thrown up in the air. He found himself walking in circles in front of his house, trying to decide what to do. Finally, he walked back inside, and he couldn't say why but he walked out to his backyard and knocked on Layla's gate. He didn't know what he was going to say to her when she got there. He wasn't even really sure why he was there, but he was, and that was the only thing right now that it seemed he knew.

When she came out of her house into the backyard, no words were spoken. She went to him and pulled him into her arms. He took that moment to embrace her back.

"How'd it go? Are you ok?" she asked.

"Nothing is the same now. I don't know how it went because I'm still on the ride."

"I thought I would hang around just in case."

Nolan was so grateful that she was so intuitive. Again Layla had shown the characteristic that he normally didn't get shown at all: compassion and consideration. He didn't have a whole bunch of friends, and even though he was friends with Connor, this wasn't something he wanted to really share with him. Of all the people he could have called, he knew Layla would be around for him.

"You are right. I should have probably talked to my parents much earlier. Now that we have talked, or at least I've talked to my mom, I'm not sure where to go from here."

Layla leaned back and then put her hand over his forehead.

"There are no rules here, Nolan. This is all about you. What happened?"

Nolan gave her the summed-up version of everything his mother had told him, and throughout the whole of it, the only reaction he got from Layla was a nod of her head.

"Your mother was very courageous in coming to you.

I know a lot of parents that might have just gone on and let you think that they had just gotten together, and it was a good coincidence."

"I know that I should be grateful that they are being so transparent, but I don't know. She wasn't the only one keeping a secret from me. I feel like they betrayed my trust. Can you love somebody and not trust them?"

"The short answer to that is yes, but do you really want to penalize them for being honest?"

"Right now, I don't know what I want to do. Right now, it just seems like there's so much that's going on or happening or has happened, and it's all going on around me."

"Did you want to stay?"

Nolan was so tempted. Layla's eyes were wide and open, and her heart was waiting for him to take that step. In lieu of everything else that had gone on with his parents, he couldn't be the one to take advantage of anyone. Decisions had consequences. Loving someone didn't mean just fixing it temporarily. It meant doing what was best for the other person.

"I want to stay, but I know I should go."

"Remember you're not alone, Nolan. If you want to talk, it doesn't matter what time of the day or night, just knock on the door. I'll be here for you."

Nolan leaned down and placed a kiss on Layla's forehead. This was what he needed.

"Thank you, Layla."

"For?"

"For being you.

Fourteen

"I'm surprised that you came into the store today. It seems like the only thing you have time for these days is the neighbor next door," Ryan said as he put out some more finished bowls. Layla knew her brother was not in a good mood. Normally, they did everything together, and since Nolan had come into town, Ryan had kept his distance.

Layla loved her brother, but she wasn't about to tell him she had fallen in love with a man who held the fate of the whole town in his hands.

"I was at the fair, and if you thought I was shirking my duties, normally, you're the first one to let me know."

Ryan gave her a lame smile.

"I'm sorry, sis. I guess it's weird having to fight for your attention with anyone else. When I look at Nolan Taggert, he's not even someone who wants to live in a town like Inheritance Bay. I was being crabby, and I shouldn't have."

This was one of the reasons she absolutely loved

working with Ryan. It was one of the things that made her and Ryan's relationship so great. They could talk about anything. One moment they could both be mad at each other, but after they talked it out, they could go on as if nothing else had ever happened.

"No, it's on me, Ry. I have been a little neglectful of the store lately. But I'm getting myself together."

She was going to say something else, but the bell rang over the shop door, and in came Micah Hamilton. Layla wasn't ready for this today. She looked for Ryan to tell him to go take care of Micah, but Ryan had already scurried to the back.

"Ryan?"

"Oh no, sis. I think you owe me this one since you've been gone so much."

Putting on her best smile, she went to the front and stood behind the counter.

"Hello, Micah. What brings you into the store today?"

He walked around the aisles and finally made his way to the counter. When he got there, he didn't have anything in his hands. So whatever today was about, it definitely wasn't about buying product.

"I am actually here on business, Layla."

Layla thought she had a bridge she could sell somebody if that was actually true.

"What kind of business?"

"There's a dinner scheduled in Sunset Valley. It's for all of the business owners you know. Of course, I'm a member of the Commerce board, so they invited me, as well. Anyway, the whole point is that they want to go ahead and show Wealth Builders what they would be getting when they put the call center in Sunset Valley."

Layla didn't say a thing; in fact, she made sure that her smile kept intact.

"Really? I hadn't heard."

All the wild thoughts ran through her head, making her wonder if this had all been planned yesterday. Did Nolan know that he was going to have to go to this dinner and that he had already made up his mind when he came to see her last night? Maybe it explained why he was so adamant about saying that them being together and the town were two separate issues. Had she been foolish for the last hectic days of being around this man? She couldn't blame anyone but herself because Nolan hadn't actually promised her anything. He said he wanted an honest assessment of Inheritance Bay, and Layla could admit she had done that by taking him to the Spring Festival. However, it seemed as though it was all in vain.

"Well, I'm not so shocked that you haven't heard. This is really something that we're trying to keep hush-hush in Sunset Valley so that the property values don't go up from people trying to buy real estate. It's one of the problems that we want to discuss at the dinner that's coming up."

Layla had to keep thinking about cool and solid thoughts. She couldn't just run out of the store and go bang on Nolan's door. She was going to retain every ounce of professionalism that she could.

"How can I help you, though?"

"I'm looking around in your store just to see if there are some things that I would like to put in my consignment shop. I'm going to open up a store in Sunset Valley, of course, when Wealth Builders is built. All members of the commerce get a storefront on these kinds of occasions. I just wanted you to think about what items you think would look good in the store there. I'm sure that if someone buys something in Sunset, we could always refer them to come back to Inheritance Bay. That might be able to drum up a little bit more business for the area."

"Well, I want to thank you for the opportunity and for letting me know. I'll definitely go through our inventory and find out what's going to work out the best for us."

"Yes, if you make up a list, I will go through it to see what's appropriate. Also, make sure on the list you put the business-to-business discount. I think that Wealth Builders opening up their center in Sunset Valley is going to be a great thing for everyone in the surrounding areas. Don't you think so?"

Layla had to take deep breaths and let them out slowly so Micah wouldn't see them. She could honestly say that Micah didn't want to know what she was thinking right now. She just needed to get through the next ten minutes. The man was almost done gloating.

"Of course, I completely agree with that sentiment."

"Quite. Then I'll leave you to whatever you were doing, and I'll look forward to your list." Without a backward glance, Micah Hamilton walked out of the store.

Ryan came from the back of the store, looking around furtively to make sure they were alone.

"What did he want?" Then, as if Ryan had finally taken a look at her, he took a step forward and said in a firmer voice, "What happened here, Layla? Do I need to go run him down?"

"Just give me a moment, Ryan. You may have to run someone down, but it won't be him."

Hurt and a feeling of foolishness flooded her whole system, making it nearly impossible to think. The foolish feeling was snowballing into anger and rage. Had he already known this was happening when he asked if he could love somebody but not trust them? It was all so coincidental. She couldn't believe that it was all an accident.

Again, what made it so bad was that Nolan hadn't promised a thing. In fact, he had been so upfront and honest with her that, in hindsight, she had been the foolish one.

"Sis, you're going to have to talk; otherwise, I'm just going to have to go run after him and beat him anyway and not have any clue why."

Layla was so deep in her own thoughts she had forgotten that her brother was waiting on her.

"It's not Mr. Hamilton, so forget about him. Well, it's sort of about him, but not really."

"You're upset, so I need you to make clear sense for me, so I know what to do, and then later you can make woman-sense when you go speak to Carrie."

Layla wanted to curl up in a ball. All of a sudden, she thought maybe she had an idea about how Princess felt. When you thought you were with someone, who was supposed to cherish and take care of you and then come to find out that they had betrayed you. The worst betrayal is the one that you take part in.

"I have been so foolish."

"I can tell I'm not going to like where this is going,

and I have a feeling it involves your neighbor," Ryan said in a tense voice.

Layla waved him off. "It's true, Nolan is the cause, but I'm the one who did this. So you remember a couple of days ago I asked you all to be nice around Nolan?"

"Yes. I thought it was weird."

"Well, as everybody knows, Nolan came here and spoke to the mayor. What everybody doesn't know is that he was looking to put his call center for Wealth Builders somewhere, and he thought that this might be a good place."

"That would be great. What's the problem?"

"It seems as though in a couple of days, there will be a commerce dinner in Sunset Valley where they will be talking about the new center they'll be getting from Wealth Builders."

"Wow, that's a real kick. How did he find out before you?"

Layla closed her eyes and sat down in a nearby chair. How had Micah found out first? She had trusted Nolan. She had kissed that man twice. She should have known better. When she opened her eyes, her brother was kneeling in front of her waiting for her to say something. He wasn't judging her, telling her how silly she was for falling for Nolan. It was just her brother waiting to be there for her. His openness and his acceptance made the pain she felt all the deeper.

Without having to say a word, Layla fell into her brother's arms and cried on his shoulder. Ryan didn't ask for details. He just rubbed her back.

"Should I go break his legs for you?"

"No, silly," she said through her tears. "The worst of it is that I don't think that Inheritance Bay ever had a chance." When Layla sat back in her chair, Ryan stood up and gave her an odd look.

"What's up with that look?"

"Well, I don't know if the source of this information is actually the best place."

"Why would he lie?"

"I'm not saying that he did. I'm just saying that I always prefer, before going ahead and convicting a person, talking to the person we're going to convict first."

"The person I'm holding responsible was very clear and very honest when he first came. He doesn't like small towns. Sunset Valley is just big enough to suit his needs. I don't think talking to him is going to make this any better. If anything, what I think I need to do is just forget that Nolan Taggert is here and go on with our lives."

"I'm here for you. If you want, I will bring my empty stomach over to your house tonight so that you can fill it and keep your mind occupied."

"You're too good to me, Ry. No, I think I want to go home and be with me for a little bit if that's ok?"

"I guess. I don't mind holding down the fort. Doing all the things that need to be done. Making the crafts that help us support the—"

"Really, Ry?"

"Ok, I'll take care of the store. If you need me, don't forget I'm here."

"Thanks, you're the best."

On her way home, Layla replayed the events of the last days. By the time she had gotten home, she wasn't angry.

She was furious. She wasn't going to play Nolan's games anymore. The first thing she did was go to the backyard to make sure that the door was locked. She found a note on it from Nolan. He would be out of town for the next three days.

The letter was the final nail in the coffin of his guilt. That was it; her neighborly duty was done. What she needed to get started on was finding a way to forget Nolan Taggert, the man she had foolishly fallen in love with.

Fifteen

The last two nights had been meeting after meeting. As he dropped his bags in the house, Nolan could say he was happy to be back in Inheritance Bay. When he first set foot off of the plane, he thought the first thing he would want was a bed.

Now that he was back in Inheritance Bay and in his home, he had a whole different set of priorities. It was odd for Nolan to think of this place as home. Right now, it was the place that he associated with peace and calm. The most important thing he wanted to do was to see Layla. He went out to the backyard and looked over the fence, and Layla was out with Princess.

"Hey, neighbor," he said, waving to her.

"Hi."

Nolan was taken back. She didn't ask him where he had been. There was no welcoming smile that he was waiting for. Maybe she hadn't gotten the note.

"Did you get the note that I left for you?"

"Yes, I got the note and everything that went with it."

Now Nolan knew something was wrong. He was hoping that he was just going to be able to say hello to Layla, and she was going to be able to take his mind off of everything else that had gone on, but now he could see that was not going to happen. He decided he would make a tactical retreat. He was tired. He didn't want to say things he'd regret, and it looked like Layla was actually ready for a fight.

"Well, goodnight," Nolan said, thinking he would just deal with this tomorrow.

"Oh, how was your dinner in Sunset Valley?"

Nolan stopped and looked back at Layla. Had she wanted him to take her with him?

"It was the same old business as usual. They had a whole bunch of people from the commerce board there. Someone in the local restaurant catered the event, and it was nice, like so many others."

Nolan stopped and really thought about the question. "Are you on the commerce board in both towns?"

"No, I'm not."

"I guess I'm a little surprised you knew about the dinner."

"I bet you are. Well, Mr. Hamilton came into the store two days ago. You remember him, right?"

"Yes, I do. He was actually at the dinner."

"Well, he came into my store to look around to find some items that he could put in the new store he plans on opening up in Sunset Valley. It seems as though everybody has been told that Wealth Builders is building a call center in the Valley."

"Really?"

"Are you really going to deny it?"

Now he understood why Layla was upset. Obviously, the mayor of Sunset Valley had decided to tell them that he had already made his decision when nothing could be further from the truth. That was a common problem working with small towns. The mayor thought that if you held a banquet for a man, that was the same thing as signing on the dotted line, but it wasn't. The problem at hand, though, wasn't the mayor of Sunset Valley. The problem at hand was Layla had jumped the gun, and Nolan was offended. What kind of man did she think he was?

"I don't have anything to deny."

"You know, you're right. You are not the problem. I am the problem, and I was. I mean, I know you said that you didn't like Inheritance Bay and that you were just doing this for Connor, but Inheritance Bay was never even on the radar."

He could tell that Layla was hurt, and he was just too tired to be accused of something with no proof. So Nolan did what he always did when his back was against a wall; he stuck with the facts.

"I was always upfront with you on my thoughts about if Inheritance Bay would be a good place for the center."

"I thought things were going really well and that you were able to see the best parts of the town, and then Hamilton comes in and tells me this."

Nolan couldn't hear anything but her outrage and pain. Is that what these last days had been to her? Had he been taken in again? He was still trying to process all of the betrayal and lies that had been going on around his mother and his father and now this. Did she think that all the times he held her, kissed her, and walked with her on the beach were part of selling Inheritance Bay?

Had Nolan Taggert forgotten the rules? Nolan always understood that when people saw him, they saw an executive from Wealth Builders. They saw somebody that would be able to help them and their families and their towns. Had he been taken in again? Could Layla have been just like everybody else?

"So has that been what's been going on between us, Layla? You want to make sure you got the best angle for the town?"

Layla stepped back as if he had hit her. "How could you even suggest such a thing?"

"I could suggest it because you seem to be able to suggest all sorts of things about me without even asking me. I thought we had a friendship, Layla. I thought we could trust each other. When people trust each other, they give each other the benefit of the doubt, and they ask each other questions. They don't make decisions for other people."

He could feel the betrayal in the reeds from everyone just boiling in him, and he didn't want to take it all out on Layla. Some of this was because of the accusation she made as soon as he came home, but the other part of this was that he had lost something again. He had thought he had a safe haven with his father. Now he found out that his father had been part of the issue all along.

Nolan thought he had a safe haven coming back to Inheritance Bay to see Layla. Then with these unfounded accusations, she, too, ripped away his safety. He needed to take a step back. This was going above and beyond where it needed to be, and he needed to be able to think clearly before he said anything else.

"You can't talk to me about trust, Nolan. I trusted you with everything, and you just left and did whatever. You did what was best for Wealth Builders. I thought that you were going to be different than my first impression of you, but I was wrong. I can't believe that you're going to make Inheritance Bay suffer for things that your parents did to you. You are going to lump us all into one big pile and decide to get back at everybody all at once. Or maybe it's not even that. Maybe it's the fact that your mother lives in Sunset Valley. Maybe you think that this will make it all better and somehow will serve as a bridge for you and your family.

"Inheritance Bay opened its heart to you, and you ripped it out and threw it on the ground as if it was worthless. Cresswell was right. You are the Reaper."

With those words, she had plunged the final dagger into his heart.

"I'm not the Reaper here. If you want to sit on your high and mighty tower and look down on me, fine, but you should at least be honest. You could do so much more for this town, but you decided to hide. People have to be responsible when they're telling you to think about others. We all have problems, and there's no problem that you have that hasn't been solved before. You called me the Reaper, but you're the one sitting in this town watching it fall apart and waiting. While everyone else is suffering, you and your brother are doing just fine. So don't look at me, Layla. Maybe you should've listened to what I told

Cresswell. The town was already gone, and I was trying to do some good for it.

"I know you didn't ask me, but I'm going to tell you the truth now. I have no intention of putting a Wealth Builders center in Sunset Valley. They are so commercialized right now there wouldn't be enough places for our workers to even find places to live that they could afford. Where we're going to go ahead and put Wealth Builders hasn't even been finalized yet. I haven't finished looking at all the spots that were recommended. If you had asked me, I would have told you; instead, you did what I have found has happened in all small towns. You jumped the gun. You made a judgment about things I would or wouldn't do, and you didn't even want to take the time to ask me."

"Nolan—"

"It's fine, Layla. I'm so used to this. Inheritance Bay, Sunset Valley, or any other small town you can find. It's always the same story. I'm the big bad wolf coming into their town that's perfect and pristine. I'm the one killing their traditions. When in truth, I'm there trying to offer them some hope."

Nolan watched Layla swallow and let out a breath. "Thank you for clearing that up. I know that you weren't being malicious. I'm just wondering at what point were you going to tell me that Inheritance Bay wasn't for you?"

"I told you before, Layla. I never saw what was going on between us and my decision about Inheritance Bay as being connected. I'm just not built that way. Business is business, and my personal life is my personal life."

Layla nodded. "I understand. I'm not built that way,

but I get what you're saying. I think it would be best for all concerned if we just tried to be civil neighbors to one another. It seems like there are more differences between us than I thought, and I'm truly sorry about the misunderstanding."

Layla walked into her house, closed and locked the door, and Nolan closed his eyes in frustration. Small towns. With everything going on, he couldn't just jump into his car and leave. He had to come up with an answer for this thing with his parents. Was he saying that? His parents? Right now, he was going to do the thing he told everybody not to do. Go to bed and hope that it all worked itself out by the morning.

Sixteen

It had been three days and eight hours since she had made a fool of herself in front of Nolan. She had taken the time to think about what he had said. Some of his words were hurtful but had a grain of truth in them and had left Layla conflicted. She thought she would be able to leave town for a little bit, but Marjorie had called her to let her know the Spring Festival had been a grand success, and a reporter wanted to do an article on small-town festivals and how it's part of a revival.

Layla wasn't sure it was as big as Marjorie was making it, but Marjorie was determined to roll out the red carpet. The reporter was coming to a quick potluck the town was putting together, and Layla was in the supermarket to get some steaks for the event. Getting steaks made her think of Nolan. She never got to tell him that steaks were the only thing she could cook.

Then, as if he could hear her talking about him, he was in front of her in the steak aisle. "You're here?" she said, confused.

Nolan gave a wan smile. "I have to eat something, and there isn't really another supermarket to go to."

Layla nodded. "You're right. There isn't."

"Are you having a party? You've put in quite a bit of steak, unless you are just shopping for the month?" Nolan said with a raised eyebrow.

"No, no, the town is having a potluck. Did you want to go? I thought you'd be too busy to go and—"

"No, I'm free."

"Oh! Well, okay. It's at seven."

"Great. That gives me about ninety minutes. I'll come by and get you. Are you taking Princess?"

He remembered Princess. "No, I'm not. I'm going to walk her before I go to the party. She's getting braver, but I don't want to push her too much."

"I understand. You've got great instincts. Princess couldn't be in better hands."

He could still say something nice about her? Why was this man such a contradiction? Every time she looked at him, she saw a different slice of him.

"Thanks."

"You deserve it. You've saved me from shopping for dinner tonight. I'll go home and get decent for you. I wouldn't want to embarrass you—gotta shave my evil villain mustache."

Layla laughed with him. "I think it's low enough. You'll do."

"Then I'll see you at seven."

Nolan turned and left. What was she doing, and what was going on? She could admit she was wrong and had jumped to the wrong conclusion, but how could she forgive him for taking a great opportunity away from the town she loved? She had no answers, just steaks in a basket. She didn't know what was going to happen tonight, but whatever it was had broken the wall of silence between her and Nolan. In a secret part of her, she had missed him.

Nolan was a glutton for punishment. That was the only reason he was going to this potluck. But he had to admit it was great to be able to talk to Layla again. This wasn't an outing or a date. It was just a public event. There would be lots of other people there, and he wouldn't be alone with her.

With everything that had already happened between him and her, Nolan would have thought the smartest thing to do was just to stay in his house. He didn't even like going to public events. But he wanted to spend some more time with Layla.

Nolan didn't like the way they had left things between them, and this gulf of distrust and silence wore on him more than he thought it would. It did nothing for him that he knew he was right—the town was in dire straits. Nolan had an obligation to Wealth Builders, though, and he didn't take that lightly.

Over the last couple of days, Nolan had looked at it, and he probably should have told Layla that Inheritance Bay hadn't even made his top three considerations so far. Hopefully, that was water under the bridge, and they would be able to find something else to talk about tonight.

He decided to go ahead and clear out a couple of last-minute reports, and before long, the ninety minutes were gone. He managed to pull himself together, throwing his jeans on and what he hoped was a casual top and then ran through the backyard to knock on her door. It took a moment before he heard the screen door unlock, and then she came out.

This was Layla. She was wearing a long, flowing blue dress, and her hair was piled up in a bun. He knew her hair wouldn't stay in that bun for long, but he was always intrigued that she decided to put it up there anyway.

"Princess all taken care of?"

Layla smiled and nodded. "She's all taken care of."

Nolan held out his hand, but Layla hesitated for a moment before she placed her hand in his. It had been too long, and he didn't even think about the action. In one movement, he pulled her close and then kissed her at the top of her forehead. He had missed her. Nolan had missed her wit, her determination, her openness, and he had missed his friend.

They froze in each other's arms.

"Sorry," he mumbled at her forehead.

"Don't be sorry. I mean, you can be sorry tonight, or later on in the evening, but for right now, let me say I missed you."

Nolan let out a big sigh and just hugged her. "What are we—"

"Stop. This is further than I thought I was going to be able to make it tonight. I don't know what we're going to do about the rest."

On the way to the dinner, neither one of them spoke. When they were halfway there, Nolan stopped. "Where are the steaks?"

"Ryan already took them over. Don't worry about it."

"That was a close call," Nolan said.

"Talking about close calls and missing dates, when are you getting together with your family?"

"I wish I had an answer. I think I'll probably schedule something at the Turtledove Inn. It will be neutral ground, and everybody can leave and go their separate directions."

"Have you talked to your father?"

"No. I think this is the longest I've gone without talking to my dad. It's weird. He's always been my dad, but now I know he's really my dad, and now things are different."

The event was like so many other events that Nolan had been to, with one major exception. He was sitting next to Layla. It seemed as though everybody came by to say hello to her. Another thing he admired about her. There was no one too big or too small for Layla not to stop and say hello to. She had the temperament of a politician and the caring of a mother. The tables were all arranged in rows, and the dais had been set up.

It was then that Nolan started to notice that there were men walking around with cameras and interviewing people.

"Layla?"

She turned when he called her name and then looked over to where he was pointing.

"It's no worries. That's actually the reporter, Evelyn Rogers, that Marjorie invited for the evening. It seems like she wants to do a piece on festivals in small towns, and she thought this would be a great opportunity for Inheritance Bay to get some more publicity."

"That's a good call," Nolan said.

"You are always amazing me."

Nolan watched Evelyn Rogers scanning the room. He knew the moment he was spotted. He saw her coming toward him and Layla and for once wished his face wasn't known. He wasn't sure how this was going to work, but he put on his charity smile and waited for Evelyn.

"Hello, Nolan Taggert from Wealth Builders, aka the Reaper?" Evelyn said with a smile. Nolan's leg was next to Layla, and he could feel her tense.

"Tonight, I'm here enjoying a town potluck," he said.

"Are you? There are rumors going about that you are scouting towns looking to put your center in a new location. How convenient it is to find you with the potter, Layla. I feel like I've hit the jackpot."

Nolan could hear the eagerness in Evelyn's voice. He wasn't concerned about himself; he looked at Layla and wanted to see if she would avoid or deny the accusation. Once again, Layla kept him on his toes.

"Yes, Evelyn. I am Layla. I'm a resident here in Inheritance Bay, and I couldn't be prouder."

Everyone at the table turned their heads after the statement. Looking around the table, he could tell they were all shocked. He tapped Layla's leg under the table. She turned to him and gave him a full smile.

"Yes, I'm a proud resident of Inheritance Bay. You see, recently, someone told me that if I wanted to make something work, I'd find a way." She turned back to the reporter and answered a couple of other questions.

It was all disrupted when they saw Cresswell with a sign that read Evict the Reaper. Nolan looked to Marjorie and saw her face fall. All at once, he knew that this was going to be his fault. The town had done so much, and he was going to be the stain. Like a shark senses blood in the water, Evelyn called her crew over to Cresswell.

"Excuse me, excuse me, are you here for Nolan Taggert?"

Seeing he had an audience, Cresswell told his story. Evelyn turned to Layla.

"Tell us, Layla, has Inheritance Bay become the latest victim to the Reaper?"

Before she could answer, Blake from the diner stood up.

"Nolan is ours. He was here for the festival, and when Cresswell came, he stood in front of Layla to protect her. That makes Nolan part of the Bay."

Allen stood up and waved his hand. "The boy is a little slow, but he's ours. He might be the Reaper to others, but he's a neighbor here. That man attacked a woman. Who can listen to a man who does that?" Allen called out.

Nolan watched Evelyn try to get microphones to the other residents that stood up to protect him. He was humbled and at a loss for words. When Evelyn came back to him to get his closing remarks, Nolan stood up and looked around to see all the nodding heads telling him to speak. When he looked down, he saw Layla, with a watery smile, looking up at him.

"Well, Evelyn, let me say that I have been looking for a location. There are a lot of locations that would be economically better to place our center. When I look at the numbers, very few small towns could make the cut. However, Wealth Builders isn't just about money. We care about the quality of our employee's lives, as well. That's why Inheritance Bay is one of the top picks for the center."

Layla stood up and gave him a confused look. "Really? When did that happen?"

Nolan pulled her into his arms and then whispered against her ear.

"You know when you want to get something done, you find a way. Just in case you don't know. I love you, Layla Cartia."

She pulled back and looked up at him. "You tell me now?"

"Yes, in front of your family."

"You've got a way about you, Nolan."

"Let's put the icing on this cake, Layla. Will you kiss me in front of your family and make an honest man out of me? This sneaking around in the backyard is wearing on me. Besides, what will I tell my parents?"

"Enough with you! Kiss me."

Nolan pulled her into his arms and kissed her. It was the first of many for them, and Nolan was looking forward to all that Layla brought with her.

I hope you enjoyed *Love at Eagle Station*. Check out *Love at Owl's Roost*, book three in the Inheritance Bay Series.

If you'd like to get more news from me sign up to my newsletter to receive updates on new releases, sale promotions, and free books.

susanwarnerauthor.com

If you enjoyed this book, you could check out some of my other series:

Love Happens series. Sweet small-town romances that show that love could be waiting for you right around the corner.

Love Endures series. Clean and Wholesome love doesn't just happen in small towns, they can happen in cities too. Second chance love stories that prove that love endures.

Silver Fox series. Love comes to us in all stages of life. Celebrate the couples that find life after kids have grown up and sometimes even after our first loves have passed.

Love Saves series. Sweet romantic comedy where couples find out what really matters in their lives, how opposites can do more than just attract and how love can save us all.

Inheritance Bay Series. Inheritance Bay is a town that needs an influx of people to keep it from dying. A call is sent offering a second chance to former residences to come back home. The people who respond are coming to Inheritance Bay lured by the prospect of a second chance and the opportunity to leave their old lives behind. However the newcomer's to the bay will find redemption, safe harbor and in some cases an inner strength they didn't know they had. What's for sure is they'll get their inheritance of finding an unconditional love that'll last a lifetime.

Hidden Treasures. (Coming Soon) Hidden treasures is a tourist town that specializes in romantic getaways. However, there is a club of women who call themselves the Liberated Damsels. They're women who have loved and lost. Now they are regaining their independence and confidence. Walk with them as they discover that taking a chance on love is worth it if the other person can see the hidden treasure within.

susanwarnerauthor.com

50606556R00095